MURDER IN THE
HIGHLANDS

JAMES GLACHAN

MR JAMES GLACHAN

Murder in the highlands is a follow up to-
Peril in the highlands.

A FRESH START

DENISE KELLY should have been celebrating a red-letter day, Monday the 8th of May 1973 was the day she took over control of Glenfurny police station. Instead, she was nursing a hangover.

She was only going to have one glass of wine the previous night, but as she sat alone in her rented flat reflecting back on her achievements since leaving Ayrshire for the highlands she decided on another.

As she was putting the bottle back in the fridge she thought about what brought her there, 220 miles from her home town of Irvine in Ayrshire to a small town in the East Highlands. Her dirty rat of a whoremaster husband that was what, or rather who. Not words she used lightly.

They were hardly back from honeymoon when he was dipping his wick in a wee trollop of a cadet he was supposed to be mentoring on the job. Worst thing was it was in their own bed.

Job, that was the problem. She was warned not to date and certainly not marry another policeman. Did she listen? No, she thought he, she, they were different. They were the real thing.

As she thought about how stupid she had been and felt sorry for herself she decided to have a little bit more wine very quickly the bottle emptied. Then half of another one.

'Shower,' she said to herself as she walked unsteadily through to the bathroom. When the water cascaded over her body she slowly turned the temperature down until it was all cold water.

No, that wasn't helping, she decided and turned the temp. back up to its warmest setting. That didn't seem to help either.

'Tea now,' she said as she towelled herself dry.

Walking into the police station she looked every inch the Detective Sergeant who could take charge of not only the station but also the 3 officers under her charge. Not in uniform but wearing a new black trouser suit with a white blouse beneath, definitely looking the part.

This was the first time her team would all be together, then her first task was to sell them her idea of a shift rota to make sure the old Monday to Friday thinking they had used for years changed to a modern seven-day working system. Still working days, but that was the reason the staff had doubled from 2 to 4.

The kettle was already boiling. P.C. Billy Lamont, who was the longest serving officer there, was first in as ever. Denise was lucky he was there, he was supposed to be transferred to Dingwall, forced there by an unthinking personnel department and reacted by walking out on the force. Denise managed to get the move stopped and he thanked her by staying on.

Denise and Billy were drinking their first cup of the morning when the first new recruit joined them. The station front door flew open and a woman, a few years older than Denise burst in.

'Hi guys, I 'm not late, am I?' she said excitedly, as she stood looking over the counter.

'No. Well not really. Plus, you are not last. It's just gone 9 o'clock. I thought the cadet would have been here by now. Come round, we have tea first thing,' Denise said.

She lifted the counter top and walked round.

Both Denise and Billy were surprised at the way she was dressed. Her bright red hair they noticed straight away, but when she walked round to join them they saw she had wedge shoes, bright red tights, a short black leather skirt and a red boob tube beneath her black leather looking plastic coat.

Straight away Denise wanted to slate her about her dress sense. Maybe she got away with it where she worked before, but she wouldn't be doing it under her watch there in Glenfurny.

'What do you take in your tea?' Billy asked.

'Two and coo,' the newcomer said with a smile. 'By the way, I am Lindsay-Joanne Connor,' she said, sticking her hand out to shake her introduction. 'Detective Constable,' she added.

The two cops stood up and welcomed her warmly.

'What did you say you take again?' Billy asked.

Linsay-Joanne laughed. 'Two and coo. Two sugars and milk.'

Billy laughed nervously.

The door bell dinged again, and they all looked over to see a nervous looking cadet walking in.

'Hi,' she said nervously.

'You must be Susan Maxwell,' Denise said, noticing the young girl's anxiousness and trying to ease her tension.

She nodded.

'Come round, we have tea first thing,' Denise said.

Susan walked round to join them.

'What do you take?' Billy asked her.

'I don't drink tea,' she said quietly.

Billy shrugged and handed Lindsay-Joanne her mug.

'What is on the agenda today,' Lindsay-Joanne asked, after sipping he cuppa and giving Billy a thumbs up.

'Today I will talk you through the shift plan I have for the next 2 months. It will be one-to one – meetings next door in the office then we will tour the town and meet a few locals. Billy, you are finished your tea, we will go first.'

They walked through to the office. Densie sat behind the desk of the tiny office that was just a glorified cupboard. Billy sat opposite.

'How are things at home?' Denise asked. She knew his mother was disabled and he was her part-time carer.

'She is still the same. It's okay, I can work shifts, my auntie lives near us and will look in on mum when I am working at thw weekend.'

Denise handed him a plan for the following 2 months. 'It's easy to follow,' she said. 'The days with a W are work days and O are when you are off.'

Billy studied it carefully, as if it was a very important contract, instead of a simple shift plan.

'On the wall is all 4 of our shift patterns, if you want a day off when you should be working you need to ask for a swap with somebody who is off.'

Billy looked round to see a cork pinboard on the opposite wall.

'Susan will be dayshift Monday to Friday for a month or two, until we see how she settles in. Any questions?'

Billy was still looking up at the corkboard. 'I think I get it,' he said.

'Good. Well, the good news is you have tomorrow off. I know it's a bit short notice, but I only finished the shifts pattern yesterday.'

'Okay,' he said, looking at the shift list again.

'Right, when you go out tell Susan to come through. After I have spoken to her you take her a walk through the town and show her your usual beat.'

'Okay,' he said as he got up, then left.

A minute later Susan Maxwell walked through the office door, ducking as she did to avoid hitting her head.

Denise smiled. 'So, Susan, how have you found being a police officer so far?'

Susan's face flushed a bit. 'I really like it. I think it's what I expected.'

'Good. Now, I don't want to scare you off, but I have been in the force for 8 years and I have found misogyny at every level of the force. Before I came here I was based in the North of Ayrshire and I can't say too much about here in the Highlands, but my advice is to work as hard as you can.'

Susan nodded.

'Obviously as a woman I will help you and Lindsay-Joanne as much as I can. Any problems you have, with anything at all, even if it is not work-related feel free to come to me. Okay.'

Susan nodded again.

'Where are you from, Susan?'

'Inverness.'

'Right. You won't be travelling here every day, are you?'

'No. My aunt who lives here in Glenfurny, I am living with her.'

'That's good. So, the thing is the other three of us will work alternate days for the next 2 months at least. I want you to work dayshift on Monday to Fridays just now. Are you okay with that?'

Susan nodded again.

Denise never spoke, waiting until Susan said something. Anything.

'I can go home at the weekends then,' she said, with a nervous smile.

'Of course you can. Do you have a boyfriend back in Inverness?'

'No.'

Denise was tiring of an interview that was as riveting as pulling teeth. 'Right, well I have told Billy to take you out on the beat with him. He will show you around the town, tell you about some of the characters we have to deal with.'

'Okay,' Susan said, then got up to leave.

'Tell Lindsay-Joanne to come in.'

Susan left and Denise braced herself for what was about to happen.

Lindsay-Joanne walked brazenly into the office. She had taken off her jacket but still looked tarty.

'Before we talk about shifts I want to talk to you about your dress sense, or rather lack of it.' Before she could answer Denise continued her character assassination. 'I don't know where you worked before, but I will be surprised if you were allowed to walk about like a street walker. How professional will people take you looking like a ten-bob prostitute instead of a policewoman?'

Lindsay-Joanne opened her mouth to answer, but again didn't get the chance.

'I don't know how long you have been in the force, but I have been fighting misogyny every step of the way. If I walked about dressed, or rather undressed like you are I would still be walking the beat back in Irvine.'

By this time Lindsay-Joanne was sitting with her arms firmly folded across her chest, waiting for the tirade to finish.

'Well?' Denise asked, waiting for her excuse.

'If you had just asked I would have told you. I travelled up yesterday and booked into the caravan park in town. When I opened my suitcase I found the lid had come off my shampoo bottle and all my clothes were covered in it. Then I found the town closes on a Sunday, and I couldn't get the rest of my clothes washed for today. Here I am wearing the clothes I had on for travelling up here yesterday. Managed to rescue a clean pair of knickers from the mess in my case. Oh, and I wasn't early because I had to put all my clothes into the launderette at the caravan park. Okay.'

Denise looked her up and down. 'I still think your dress sense is a bit on the common side even if you were off duty yesterday when you travelled up.'

Lindsay-Connor sighed before continuing. 'For the past 6 months, every Monday to Friday I have been wearing my most boring clothes day-in day-out, so at the weekends when I am off work I like to dress like a woman. If you think I look cheap, well maybe I am, but one thing it won't do is stop me being a good policewoman when I am working. If at any time you think my work standard is less than you expect then then we can talk about it.'

Denise felt rotten for jumping to conclusions, but her pride stopped her from apologising.

'What about the shoes? Not much good for walking the beat, are they?' she said, trying another angle.

'Normally on the first day at a new station it's just an

induction. Didn't expect to be walking the beat.'

'Well, you will find this is not a normal station, not a normal town. I had planned to take you and Susan round the town to meet a few locals. Walking of course. Now Susan is off with Billy leaving me with you. Anyway, the reason we are here is to talk about the new shift pattern.'

Denise handed over her shift pattern.

'As I said to Billy if you need one of your scheduled days off then you will need to swap.'

Lindsay-Joanne looked at the pattern with as much scrutiny as Billy had before she spoke. 'What is this all about?'

'You were told we would be working alternate days to cover the weekends, weren't you?'

'No.'

'No?'

'No. I was just told you needed cover here.'

'Well, how do you feel about working weekends?'

'I am 26, single and very much looking for a man in my life. Something it will be hard for me to do in this backwater on a Tuesday night.'

'How do you mean a Tuesday night?'

'Well, if I am off on a Wednesday I will be going out on a Tuesday night. I don't expect there is much action at the local nightclub on a Tuesday night.'

Denise laughed. 'No, we don't have a nightclub.'

Lindsay-Joanne looked at her angrily then laughed. 'Is there a bingo hall then?'

Denise laughed again. 'No. Not even a cinema.'

'What do you do on your nights off then?'

'Usual stuff, washing, ironing and drinking wine.'

'The wine drinking sounds ok.'

They both laughed again.

'So, what do you want to do? Work the weekends or get onto personnel and get a move elsewhere?'

'Well, I have paid for the caravan for a month. So, I suppose I might as well stay.'

SUNDAY, SUNDAY

SUNDAY MORNING and Denise was on duty with Billy. They checked the log from the night before. Glenfurny was only manned during the day, any call outs at night were handled by the main office in Dingwall.

Any callouts were recorded in a log book in the porch of the station. All there had been was a fight outside the Pheasant Plucker pub. Two men were arrested but were too drunk to even give their names.

Denise read the log book while Billy sorted the tea. She made a mental note to go to the pub in the afternoon after 12:30 when it opened to find out who the drunk fighters were.

'Wee treat for breakfast,' Billy said, then unwrapped an old plain loaf wrapper to reveal two lumps of home-made dumpling.

'It's a bit early,' Denise said, until the spicy aroma hit her nose. 'Maybe not,' she said, changing her mind.

They were just finished their treat when the phone rang.

'We never get a minute,' Billy said seriously.

Denise laughed. The day before they had only been disturbed twice on the whole shift. 'I'll get this one,' she said, going over to answer the phone.

'Glenfurny,' was all she got out. The voice on the other end of the phone was rattling words out ten to the dozen.

'Okay. Where did it happen?'

By the time she put the phone down Billy was the other side of the counter with the police Ford Escort's keys in his hand.

Denise put the phone down. 'Billy where's the A949?' She knew all the roads around the town by name, not by number yet.

'That's the main road south out of town. What is it?'

'Car smash. Somebody's trapped in the car, fire brigade and ambulance are on their way.'

'Am I driving?'

'Yes, but not like Miss Daisy,' Denise said. When Denise arrived a few months before their squad car was a decrepit Morris Minor and Billy drove like a geriatric woman. With the Ford Escort he was a bit faster.

The car sped through the town streets and out south. Denise felt an increasing feeling of dread. Not because of Billy's driving, she hated the road since an incident earlier in the year when she crashed her beloved car, a Hillman Avenger, the yellow peril as she had always called it because of its colour.

'Any idea exactly where the crash is?' Billy asked. He had a smile on his face as he drove the cop car as fast as he dared on the narrow and winding country road.

'The 999 operator said it was about halfway between here and Dingwall.'

The smile slipped off Billy's face. He was sure they were headed for the exact spot where his boss had crashed. He knew, or at least had an idea, how badly it had and would affect her again.

He was right, as they neared the spot Denise had the same feeling of impending doom. As they headed round to the top of the hill, and the crash site appeared it was a sinking feeling of déjà vu. The crashed car was a Hillman Hunter that had smashed head first into the tree just a bit further down the hill from the one Denise had hit.

There were 2 other cars parked and the owners out trying to help.

'Put the car in front of those cars and try to keep the road clear, Billy,' Denise ordered.

Billy stopped the car in the middle of the road 20 yards from the nearest car and put both the hazard warning and blue flashing lights on.

Adrenalin kicked in, as soon as the car stopped Denise was out and rushing up the road. She had a bit of First Aid knowledge and hoped she could help, if only a little bit.

The car's passenger door was open and an elderly woman in her 60's was clearly in distress. There was a woman tending her.

'She is okay,' the woman said calmly. 'Mostly shock and worry about her husband. We are nurses. Her husband is trapped behind the wheel and unconscious. Caroline there is also a nurse.'

Denise looked over and saw a stunning looking woman and ignored the fact she was told twice she was a nurse. She hurried round and looked through the partially open door. She couldn't see through the windscreen, it was shattered.

The driver was unconscious. Terry, the nurse was talking to him and patting his hand.

'How is he?' Denise asked.

'He is unconscious, but his vitals are okay. Problem is, he is trapped by the legs. The impact on the tree has forced the engine back.'

Their chat interrupted with what sounded like 2 different sirens approaching quickly.

'Okay. Do you know what happened?'

'No. It was like this when we arrived.'

'Thanks,' Denise said before leaving to talk to the other couple who were waiting by their car.

As she walked round she saw there was a queue forming as Billy worked hard at directing traffic before the ambulance and fire brigade arrived and would then close the road.

The couple waiting beside the front car looked pale and scared.

'Did you see what happened?' Denise asked.

The guy, who was probably in his late 20's swallowed hard before answering.

'Yes, he nearly hit us. We came over the brow of the hill and I hit the brakes gently. I knew the road was steep and you built up speed as you went down it. Plus, I remembered there was another smash here a few months ago.'

Denise closed her eyes and tried to shake the thought of the accident out of her mind.

'On the other side of the road on the hill opposite there was an old tractor going down the hill then I saw this car,' he said, pointing to the light green car wedged against the tree. 'It was speeding down the hill. I thought he was going to hit the tractor. I slowed down to nearly a stop as I could see the green car was going to come over to my side of the road. He shot past the tractor then to avoid hitting us he pulled over and smacked into the tree.'

For a moment Denise had to compose herself. It sounded exactly like what happened to her. Had this guy's brakes been tampered with?

'Do you think he took ill?' she asked.

The other driver shook his head. 'Looked like brake failure to me.'

'Yes, it sounds like that's possible, but we can't jump to conclusions. I will need a statement from you when we get this

15

cleared up.' She took their names, phone number and the car's registration then said they could go if they wanted.

Without delay they got in the car and drove off.

The ambulance arrived first and parked up where the other car had been. Just behind them was the police car from Dingwall. Another distant siren signalled the fire brigade was nearby to.

Denise walked over and told the other 2 uniforms what had happened. Then she checked with the ambulance crew. The nurse that stopped had been right, the woman was just in shock and was being attended by one of the ambulance crew.

 As soon as they could they got the woman out. Denise heard the medic call her Mrs. Cameron. She took a mental note of it. She also thought she recognised her face, so she probably lived in Glenfurny.

The fire engine pulled up behind all the other cars and the crew quickly got out and assessed the situation. Next they had their pneumatic gear out and were attacking the roof of the car to get the trapped driver out.

The lead fireman walked over to Denise.

'You in charge?' he asked.

'Well, I am the highest ranked officer here, so I suppose so.' She knew that as the accident was assessed it might change to something other than an accident and be moved away from her jurisdiction.

'Getting the roof off is the easy part. It will depend how he is jammed in by the car's bodywork, but he will be out shortly.'

Five minutes later the groaning man was stretchered away into the waiting ambulance. Fifteen minutes after that the emergency services were gone, leaving Billy, Denise and the other two cops to clear the last of the traffic.

Billy walked over to Denise. 'Is that us finished?' he asked.

'Yes, let's get back to the station.' The other uniforms were waiting for the recovery lorry to take the smashed car back to the police garage in Dingwall.

She looked at her watch before she got in the car, after one o'clock. 'Lucky we had that dumpling earlier to sustain us. Let's get back for some lunch.'

Back in the car, Billy had to drive up the hill to turn around to head back to Glenfurny. As they drove past the crash site Denise turned and looked around.

'That must have been the last thing you wanted to see,' Billy said.

'I have had to drive past here more regularly than I would want to. Now I will be thinking of the poor guy who looks as if he has been badly injured when I pass this way, at least I got off lightly.'

Although she said it, they both knew she was kidding herself.

NEXT DAY

THE FOLLOWING day Denise was supposed to be off, but she was tasked with interviewing the Cameron's about the accident. As the panda car was needed by D.C. Connor and the cadet Susan Maxwell she needed to use her own car. The bright yellow Hillman Avenger, that she inherited from her father, had been fine after being sorted after the crash.

She decided to arrive at the hospital around 11 o'clock, after the doctors had finished their rounds and before visiting times. There was the possibility the nurses could be jobsworths, but the threat of a charge of wasting police time usually changed attitudes.

The Ross Memorial hospital was a collection of Victorian buildings but with modern signposts. Denise quickly found the reception area.

In her pocket she held her warrant card. 'Hi. I am Detective Sergeant Denise Kelly from Glenfurny police station. I am here to interview Mr. and Mrs. Cameron who were involved in a car accident yesterday.'

'Oh yes. We were told somebody would be round today. If you wait I can get one of the Doctors to tell you how they are doing. Take a seat.'

Denise sat on one of the cheap looking plastic seats opposite the desk and waited. She wondered if the doctors were as old as the buildings.

A few minutes later the Doctor appeared in front of her.

'Are you here to see about the date you owe me?' he said.

Denise looked up to see Doctor Grant Jameson, the medic who checked her out when she was assaulted just after she arrived in the Highlands. He reminded her she owed him a date. Since then, events had conspired to have her forgetting all about men. When she saw him standing in front of her a deep yearning growled inside her. She fancied him the first time she laid eyes on him. Months later he looked even sexier.

'No,' she said smiling. 'The Cameron's. They were brought in yesterday after a car crash.'

'Always business with you Denise,' he said, smiling back at her.

Denise swallowed; he remembered her name.

'Mrs. Cameron has slight concussion; she can go home today. Mr. Cameron has two broken legs and bruised ribs. He was operated on last night and will be in for a couple of weeks.'

'Good. Can you take me to see them or point me in the right direction.'

'They are in different buildings. We can go to the women's ward first.'

He walked out first then held the door open for her. They walked slowly across the gravel car park.

'So, what about that date?' he asked.

'It could be a problem. I am working shifts now. I haven't got my shift pattern with me.'

'You are not saying no then?'

'No. I mean yes. Oh, you know what I mean.'

'That's a yes then.'

'Yes. Well, it depends where you are going to take me.'

'I think I can stretch to dinner in the Highland Hydro Hotel here in Dingwall.'

Denise was impressed, the Highland Hydro was the top-rated hotel in the area. It would take her a weeks wages to pay for a dinner there. 'You will need to phone the station on Wednesday, I will have my shift pattern there.'

She didn't know why she was playing so hard to get, they both fancied each other, they were both available. Something about him seemed too good to be true, maybe that was the reason she was being a bit coy.

They reached the female block and once again the Doctor led the way. They found Mrs. Cameron in a ward at the rear of the hospital.

'You look a lot better than the last time I saw you,' Denise said by way of introduction.

'Sorry, dear. I don't remember.'

Denise's heart sunk. Sounded like she had amnesia, and she had wasted a trip. Well, maybe not wasted altogether.

'Your face does seem familiar,' the old lady said.

'I am Detective Constable Denise Kelly. I am based at Glenfurny, and I was at the site where you had the accident. Can you talk me through what happened yesterday?'

She held her breath, hoping Mrs. Cameron remembered what happened.

'Yes, of course I do. It was just yesterday; I am not losing my marbles altogether. Now we were going to Dingwall to meet my sister and her man for lunch. As usual we were running late, and Johnny was going too fast. When we went over the hill I told him to slow down. Johnny suddenly went- oh oh. I ask what it was, he said the brakes weren't working. His foot went down to the floor, and nothing happened. He pulled on the handbrake and still nothing. In fact, because of the steep hill we were actually picking up speed. There was a tractor near the bottom of the hill on our side and a car heading down on the other side of the road.

We were going to crash. I knew it and he knew it. He blasted on his horn to warn the tractor driver, hoping he would pull over. He didn't. We crossed to the other side of the road and passed the tractor. The other car on that side of the road was coming straight for us. Johnny pulled onto the grass verge. Then bang.'

There was a silence after that as it sank in. Denise recalled her own accident and the chilling parallels between the two. She realised how lucky she had been, she walked out of it unscathed. At least physically.

'Sorry Mrs. Cameron, I haven't even asked you your first name.'

'Oh, right dear. It's Mabel.'

'This has all been terrible for you Mabel.'

'Yes. I'm so worried about Johnny. You know he is seventy-two and never been in a hospital before.'

'Wow, that's amazing. Anyway, I need to go and see your husband now. Take care and I will pop in and see you when you get home.'

'Okay dear. Tell Johnny I will see him soon. I am getting out later, I can visit him this afternoon.'

Grant led Denise out of the building and along to the male only building next door.

Johnny Cameron was sleeping when they approached his bed.

'Denise. I think you should leave the room just now.'

'What?'

He reached across and felt the man's brow.

'I saw him an hour ago and he was better looking than this.'

Denise did as asked, and as she looked back she saw the curtain being pulled round the bed.

As she left the ward there was a panic as another Doctor and nurse shot past her.

Denise stood looking through the window into the ward. Johnny had taken a turn for the worst she was sure of that, it seemed serious.

Ten minutes later one of the Doctor's left the curtained enclosure with his head down. The nurse followed then Grant himself appeared. He looked up and saw Denise and gently shook his head.

Denise felt sorry for the family, more so for poor Mabel who wasn't at her husband's side when he passed away.

Doctor Jameson walked over to her. 'It was peaceful in the end,' he said.

'Shame his wife wasn't at his side.'

'Yes, it was all so quick.'

'What do you think it was that killed him? Heart attack?'

'My guess it was a blood clot. With the trauma of the crash and his trapped legs then clots are often caused.'

'Well, I am glad it's not me that has to break the bad news to Mabel,' Denise said.

Just at that the Doctor was called away by one of the nurses. Denise took her chance to get away. Hospitals were never her favourite places to be.

ACCIDENT? WHAT ACCIDENT

DENISE WAS on duty with Susan Maxwell, the cadet, three days after the accident on the Wednesday. She was reading over the report she had written up when the office phone rang.

Susan answered it as she saw her boss was busy.

'Hello. Yes, she is here. Hold on.'

Denise looked up inquiringly. She wasn't happy when the cadet just shrugged. Walking over she looked at her disappointedly as she took the handset from her. She had told her more often than she should have needed to about phone manner, what to say when she answered and what it was about in case she herself could help.

'D.S. Kelly. How can I help.'

Denise listened as the Detective Inspector Morton from Dingwall told her the brakes on the Hillman Hunter had failed because the garage had used inferior parts. It was serviced and MOT'd at Brown's garage locally in Glenfurny, the paperwork was still in the car.

With the death of Mister Cameron, the crash was no longer being classed as an accident and the garage owner, Freddy Brown, was being investigated.

Denise was angry because she had taken her car there in the past. However, her car had been checked at the police garage in Dingwall when she had crashed it.

What the D.I. needed now was her reports. As the fax machine at the station had packed in again she would have to take them personally over to Dingwall. She told Morton that, even though she would need to drive past the crash site again.

Hanging up, she took a breath before turning to Susan. Right then wasn't the time to reprimand her over her phone technique.

'Right Susan, I need to go to Dingwall with some paperwork. You can either come with me or hold the fort here?'

Susan thought about it. 'It's quiet here, I would rather go with you.'

'Right, let's go,' Denise said as she got the keys for the Escort. 'Oh, remind me to phone them about the fax machine when we get back. Hasn't worked properly since they put it in.'

Susan nodded then followed her boss out of the station.

DING- DONG

DENISE DROVE the cop car faster than she would her own car. It was newer and more powerful than her older Avenger.

As she drove Denise found she having to start any conversation as she tried to find out more about her colleague and try to break down the barriers between ranks.

The first time Susan spoke was when Denise slowed the car as they went down the hill just before the crash site.

'Is this where the car crashed?' she asked.

Denise swallowed. 'Yes.'

She had to give the car a little more gas as they headed back up the hill. There was no other traffic in sight, so Denise decided to stop opposite the damaged tree that had stopped the Hillman Hunter in its tracks.

She looked round and saw Susan was looking in awe at the large pine tree, its bark bared and disfigured, unlike the others in the forest.

'Must have hit it with some force,' she eventually said.

'Yes. The driver was trapped by the legs.'

'Was he badly hurt?'

'Yes, he passed away. Initially he had two broken legs and bruised ribs. That's why my reports are suddenly more important.

Looks like our local garage supplied him with cheap brake parts that failed. The case has now been taken off out hands.'

'That's such a shame. Just driving along then this happens. It's a pity we haven't got the case, it sounds like something to get our teeth into.'

'Yes,' Denise said, then drove on, looking straight ahead, choosing not to look at the tree she hit just up from the smashed pine.

'Do you think they will cut the tree down?'

'I would think so. Plenty firewood in that big thing. Plus, if it fell it would cause a lot more damage.'

The rest of the journey was carried on in relative silence, as Denise had given up prompting Susan for the time being. Also, in the back of her mind she reflected on how lucky she had been when she crashed the yellow peril.

At Dingwall police station Denise led the way to the C.I.D. department. She flashed her warrant card at the front desk and said she was looking for D.I. Morton. The receptionist started to explain the way, but Denise waved her away, she knew where she was going, having been there before.

She found the Detective sitting in the detective pool. She presumed it was him; he was the only one there and she hadn't been told he was out.

'Detective Inspector Morton?' she asked when they were close enough for conversation.

The cop looked round his mouth broke into a big smile, looking at the two good-looking women. 'At your service,' he said.

'Detective Sergeant Denise Kelly, cadet Susan Maxwell. You phoned me earlier about the crash halfway between here and Glenfurny. This is the file I had prepared.'

The Inspector smiled. 'You could have faxed it,' he said, his gaze flitting from one woman to the other as he wondered if the women had an ulterior motive.

Denise seemed to read his mind. The guy had short, cropped brown hair that looked more plucked than trimmed. His eyebrows looked like 2 black caterpillars. He was wearing thick, black-rimmed glasses, sat on a big nose with a similarly thick black moustache on his top lip. His lips looked like they were sculpted from foam rubber. If he were the last man on Earth Denise would turn to women.

'Our brand-new fax machine hasn't worked since they installed it, otherwise we would have saved ourselves a round trip here.'

Morton was already checking over the report and nodding his head. 'Good work Denise. Or was it you Susan who wrote this up?'

Denise felt like she needed a sick bucket as this neanderthal of a cop was so like many she had encountered over the years in her career who felt it okay to be so patronising.

Denise looked over at Susan, expecting her to be tongue-tied. She got a surprise.

'No, sir, I wasn't working on Sunday. It's all the boss's own work. I think you will find it very accurate.'

Denise held back a smirk. It wasn't what she said, it was the way Susan had said it.

'Anyway, we need to get back to Glenfurny. Things to do,' Denise said, keen to get away from the creepy misogynist.

'Yes, there must be sheep out on the road by now,' Morton said sarcastically.

'Actually, we just got word of a hit-and-run. That's why we need to get back,' Susan said.

With that they turned and hurried away.

'When I am in the town I will call in at the station,' Morton called after them.

'If you really must,' Denise called back to him.

Before heading back to Glenfurny they headed out to the police garage at the rear of the complex. Johnny Cameron's Hillman Hunter was in what seemed to be a thousand bits, all forensically examined by the police mechanics.

As they stood looking the head mechanic walked over. 'Mess isn't it,' he said.

'Yes. He was lucky he didn't die at the scene,' Denise said. 'Got him eventually.'

'Yes, we heard that. Looks like this will be a murder investigation, all the top brass have been down here.'

'It was horrific, I was at the crash scene. Hope who caused it pays for it. Anyway, we need to get back.'

Denise nodded gently to Susan, and they walked slowly away.

AN ANGRY MAN

DENISE TURNED to Susan before starting the panda car.

'I will give you a bit of advice I learned the hard way. The Scottish police force we are working in is a man's world. To be treated as equals, or close to it, we need to work much harder than any man of a similar rank to us.'

Susan nodded gently, taking it in.

'Never think sleeping with a senior officer will help you up the ladder. It will only get you up the duff.'

Susan was puzzled. 'Up the what?'

'Up the duff. Pregnant.'

'Is that what happened to you?'

'No. I got where I am today by working harder than anybody else I know. No, where I went wrong was I married another cop. Oh, I was warned. It will never work; he will cheat with another officer behind my back.'

'Did he?'

'Yes he bloody did. The ink was barely dry on our marriage certificate when he was sleeping with a cadet under his care. In my own bed which made it worse, if that was possible.'

'Sounds horrible.'

'It was. Anyway,' she said as she started the car, 'we better get back to this hit-and-run you heard about.'

Both women laughed before Denise drove away, heading back to Glenfurny.

Back at the police station they hardly got to the front door when a car door slammed shut in the car park.

The driver was stomping across the car park in their direction. Denise ignored him and walked into the office.

As soon as he was in the office she raised his voice angrily. 'What's going on with my father's car?'

Denise quickly worked out it was Johnny Cameron's car, and the irate man was obviously his son.

'Mister Cameron is it?' Denise asked.

'Yes. Why can't the police garage released dad's car to the insurance company?'

'The thing is Sir, the inquiry into your father's accident is still ongoing.'

'Why?'

'The mechanics aren't happy with what they found,' Denise answered, being as diplomatic as she could.

'He had it serviced and MOT'd last week, how could there be anything wrong with it?'

'I am not a mechanic. As far as the investigation goes it's been handed to Detective Inspector Morton at Dingwall headquarters. You will need to contact him for further information.'

'Fucking Freddy Brown!' Mr. Cameron's snarled loudly. 'It's Brown, isn't it. Bet you he is putting dodgy parts in cars again. Well, is he?'

'As I said, you will need to ask Detective Inspector Morton,' she repeated.

'Fuck,' was all he said, raging at her as he turned then stormed out. As he went out he tried to slam the office's front door only to be foiled by the door closer.

Denise watched out the window as he stomped back to his

car.

'Right, Susan, question for you. If the mechanic who worked on the car messed up, what could he be charged with?'

Susan covered her eyes as she thought.

'Come on, you are just out of cop training school, it should be fresh in your mind.'

Susan clicked her fingers. 'Manslaughter due to lack of care and attention.'

'Right, and the possible sentence?'

'It could be as much as life in prison, although that would be an extreme case.'

'Well done. Now, get the kettle on.'

DOCTOR, DOCTOR

DENISE HAD just finished her tea when the phone rang. She nodded to Susan to answer and try her new phone manner.

'Glenfurny police station. How can I help?'

Denise smiled at the improvement.

Susan turned and offered her the phone. 'The Doctor,' was all she said.

Denise wondered what she meant and walked over and took the phone from her.

'Hello,' she said.

'Is that the sexiest policewoman in Glenfurny?'

Doctor Grant Jameson. She had forgotten he was going to call to arrange their date. 'Listen, I can't talk just now. Call me back in 30 seconds.'

Denise put the phone down. When she turned to Susan, the cadet had a big smile on her face.

'What?' Denise asked.

'He asked if I was the sexiest policewoman in Glenfurny. I guessed it was for you.'

Denise sighed. Although she wanted to know about her staff there were parts of her personal life she preferred to keep to herself. 'I need to take the call in the office.'

Susan raised an eyebrow.

'I need to check the shift rota if you must know. I need to

make an appointment.'

Susan just nodded. 'Appointment, right.'

The phone was already ringing when Denise walked into the back office. 'Hi.'

'Are we still on for our dinner date?'

'Yes.' She was being coy, but her heart was almost missing a beat. She fancied the pants off the Doctor, but something just wasn't clicking.

'You don't sound enthusiastic.'

'Well, we haven't spoken about girlfriends or boyfriends for that matter.'

'I haven't got either. What about you?'

'No. I have an ex-husband who is miles away and will never be in my life again. No boyfriend.'

'Well then, does that make you more enthusiastic?'

'Right, let me look at my shift pattern. How does the 24th of June suit?'

'Oh, that's a fortnight away. Is that your first available day?'

It wasn't. She was making sure she had a two-day break, just in case, well, she thought, just in case they stayed over.

'Yes. Busy, busy, busy.'

'Right 24th it is. I will book it and get back to you nearer the time.'

'Okay. Look forward to it.'

'Bye.'

'Bye-bye,' she said and put the phone down. As she did so she imagined him running his hands over her welcoming body. It was, she realised, too long since she had seen any action.

AN INSPECTOR CALLS

THE FOLLOWING Tuesday Denise was on duty with Billy and Susan. She had sent them out on the beat, getting the cadet used to the locals and their ways.

The office door opened followed by a gentle tapping on the counter. Denise looked up. D.I. Morton looked back, smiling lasciviously.

A shiver ran down her spine.

'Inspector Morton. To what do I owe this pleasure?'

'I was bringing back Freddie Brown from his interview. We don't have enough to charge him yet but it's only a matter of time.'

'What is his side of the story?'

'He is blaming the supplier. Whatever the story we have the paperwork, his account, MOT, the lot. Mr. Cameron was charged full price for cheap, defective parts. Minimum he will be charged is with fraud, but we will be going for more than that.'

As he spoke he was constantly looking at her and licking his lips. Denise thought he looked like a lizard. Or a giant snake. She just hoped he would be away before Susan walked back in.

'Good oh. Well, it's nice to see you.'

'The thing is, I was wondering if you fancied going out for a drink one night?'

Denise smiled, only if it had strychnine in it she thought.

'Sorry, but I have a boyfriend.'

'Oh, I thought you were divorced.'

'No, not yet. Separated, but I have another guy on the go.'

'Oh, right. Is the other girl not here?'

'What Susan, the cadet? No, she is out on the beat.' Denise felt her blood start to boil at the thought of this old lech wanting to date a young girl under twenty years old.

'Oh, just wanted to praise her for standing up to me the other day. Brave, it showed guts.'

That took the wind from her sails. She was ready to rip into him, now it was quite the reverse.

'Oh, well I will tell her when I see her.'

'Yes. Okay, well then I will get out of your hair. I can see you are busy.'

Once again Morton managed to grate with Denise.

'Yes, we have a serious knicker nocker. Somebody is stealing underwear from clothes lines. You know the same as me that people start like that and soon they are sexually assaulting women if we don't nip this in the bud.'

Morton, for the first time, looked impressed with the Detective Constable.

'Good. Let me know how you get on.'

With that the D.I. left the police station and Denise went back to her notes.

DOCTOR, DOCTOR

DENISE GOT off the bus opposite the Highland Hydro and walked towards the entrance. She thought about driving the 5 miles or so from Glenfurny, but she planned on having a drink or two.

The days since she arranged the date seemed to drag and at least once a day she wondered how the night would go. Sometimes she imagined them falling out over something stupid, other times they ended up in bed together and having mind blowing sex.

As she reached the car park she saw the Doctor's sports car parked up. He was there, that was a start. Another time she imagined him dizzying her and not turning up. Not tonight.

The smell as she approached the restaurant reminded her she hadn't eaten since noon, seven hours previously. Still with the Hydro's reputation she was sure she would get her fill that night. Maybe in more ways than one.

As she spoke to the maître de at the restaurant's entrance, Doctor Jameson saw her and hurried over from his window seat.

'She is with me Martin,' he said politely as he reached his date. With that he took her hand and kissed it gently.

'Madam.'

Denise felt her cheeks redden slightly, hoping nobody had witnessed it, but liking it just the same.

'Over here at the window,' he directed her, taking her by the hand.

As they sat down he clicked his fingers. When the waiter saw him Grant signalled, and the waiter just nodded.

'Champagne okay?' Grant said.

'What girl doesn't love champagne.'

Denise looked and saw what lovely eyes he had. She hadn't noticed they were green. Not bright, just lovely. He had short hair, not cropped, but tight and cut in a way that suited him.

He was fit looking, probably a gym freak. Denise thought that was a waste of energy, she knew other ways to burn off excess energy.

The champagne was cold and slipped down too easily. Denise knew she would have to pace herself, especially as she hadn't anything in her stomach.

The menu was outstanding and the amount of choice a bit staggering to Denise.

'Tell you what, you said you could read people, you order for me,' Denise challenged him.

'Okay, but you won't know what the food is until they bring it through.'

'Deal,' she said and reached a hand out. Grant shook it, the touch sending a spark through Denise's body.

The waiter brought their starters. He placed a prawn cocktail in front of Denise, Grant got pate.

'Wrong,' Denise said. 'Hate fish.'

'Prawns aren't fish,' Grant corrected.

'They smell like fish, taste like fish so if they aren't fish they are doing a good impression of a fish.'

'Okay, swap. I have chicken liver pate.'

'Wow, my favourite.'

True to form, Grant got the main course wrong as well.

However, for the dessert he ordered both sticky toffee pudding.

Denise was nearly impressed. 'I suppose one out of three is okay.'

Denise emptied the last of her champagne after finishing her food.

'So, what do we do now?' Grant asked with a twinkle in his eye.

'It's still early, we could go out to the sun lounge and watch the sun go down,' Denise suggested.

'Okay, you grab a seat, and I will get more drink.'

Instead of sitting in the lounge, Denise headed to the outdoor seats. The sun was setting as Denise sat down outside. There was a cool breeze blowing off the water. As she sat down she smiled. It was the first time in years she felt really content.

Grant appeared with another bottle of champers and two glasses.

'If I have another glass I will be under the table,' Denise joked.

'What would you be with two glasses?' Grant laughed.

'Time will tell.'

By the time they had finished the second bottle it was dark, and the chill was starting to bite.

'Listen Denise, we have had a great night. I think we get on and it's too early to go home.'

'What are you saying?'

'How about I see if they have a room for the night?'

'Twin room?'

'If you want, but a double would be cosier.'

'Okay, you go see.'

Grant left for reception as Denise pulled her jacket close to keep the cold out. She licked her lips; her best possible outcome of her dreams was about to come true.

Grant appeared a few minutes later, shaking a key on a large wooden keyring. 'Come on, room 13, hope it's not your unlucky number.'

Densie smiled. She was sure from now on it would be her lucky one.

Densie woke at some time during the night. It was pitch black and for a few seconds she wondered where she was. The realisation that she was naked, and the bold Doctor was lying next to her snoring brought the memory of the night before back.

She lay smiling, her hand reached down between her legs. She would, she knew, be sore later when she had to pee, but it was worth it. Doctor Grant Jameson knew his way around a woman's erogenous zones without a map.

His foreplay had her almost screaming in delight, the sex had her moaning madly in ecstasy. She realised then that she had fallen asleep without even washing. She thought about getting up but drifted off to sleep again.

Sometime later she woke again. This time she knew exactly where she was. Grant was lying on his back, breathing gently, the snoring stopped.

She thought back over the last two years. Her father had died, leaving her an orphan in her twenties. The sadness of that blown away by her romance and later marriage to D.S. John Kelly. Then that was quickly ruined putting her back to a major low.

The chance to move to the highlands had been a whirlwind, assault and being in danger eclipsed by getting the promotion she deserved. Now it seemed she had the perfect man.

She turned round and put an arm over Grant's chest before

falling asleep, dreaming of more sex in the morning.

The loud beeping of the alarm woke her for a third time. Realising she was in the hotel bed she looked round to see Grant up and on the phone.

'Okay. Right, I will be there as soon as I can,' he said. He turned to Denise looking disappointed. 'That was the hospital paging me. They have an emergency and need me right away.'

As he walked over she admired his naked body. She ached for him to climb in beside her and love her. Instead, he quickly kissed her and started looking for his clothes that were quickly discarded the night before.

'Don't worry, I will pay the bill on the way out. I will pay for the breakfast too, so have something to eat. I will phone you next week.'

As soon as he was dressed he reached below the bed for a small suitcase. He turned and blew her a kiss and was off.

He had a suitcase, that didn't add up to Denise. Unless he was so confident they would end up spending the night together. She shook her head. 'Cocky sod,' he said to the empty room.

After showering she had a dilemma, put the dirty panties back on or go without. Commando, she decided and stuck the pants in her small handbag.

After a lovely full Scottish breakfast Denise was ready to take on the world. Feeling great she walked up to reception to hand over the room keys.

The receptionist smiled as she checked the register.

'Doctor Jameson's room. Are you getting nervous?'

'No.'

'Well, it is only two months until the wedding.'

Denise didn't need to be a detective to work out she had just been played. He hadn't lied to her when he said he hadn't a girlfriend all right, he had a fiancée.

'I am sure I will be nearer the time,' Denise said, keeping her cool and walking out of the hotel with her head held high.

Heading back to Glenfurny on the bus Denise was steadily getting angrier with herself. Not him, the dirty shit that he was, but herself. How gullible. Not to check with anyone who could vouch that the Doctor was available.

She decided to head straight to the police station. Billy and Lindsay-Joanne were on duty so he had no worries that they couldn't cope with anything. Her main reason for going there was to use the phone to check if the Doctor had really been called out on an emergency. She doubted it very much.

As the bus headed up toward the cop shop it was held up.

Denise could see flashing blue lights up ahead. Looking through the windscreen of the bus she saw an ambulance outside Brown's garage and the panda car double parked next to it.

She got up and walked to the front of the bus. 'Could you open the doors, I need to get out.'

'I can't let you out until we get to the bus stop at the top of the road.'

'I am a police officer.'

'Yes, and I own the bus company. I just drive the bus as a hobby.'

Denise was raging. She went into her handbag and rooted for her warrant card. Finding it she was careful not to pull her panties out along with it.

She thrust it in front of the driver. 'Okay, open the door or I will report you.'

Panicking, the driver quickly hit the lever, and the door slowly opened letting Denise jump out.

Up at the garage Billy was directing traffic. Lindsay-Joanne was at the double doors at the front of the garage.

'What's happened?' Denise asked.

'Looks like the van has slipped off it's axel support and trapped somebody.'

Denise looked in and saw two ambulance men waiting to check on the poor trapped guy. At the front of the van somebody, Denise guessed was a mechanic, was frantically working a jack to raise the vehicle.

Suddenly an anxious looking woman ran up towards the garage.

'Is it Freddie? Is it Freddie?' she was screaming.

'You see to her,' Denise said, walking into the garage to see how the mechanic was doing.

As she neared the front of the van she could see it slowly inching upwards. When it was clear of the body one of the medics leaned in.

He turned round and shook his head slowly. He was dead.

Denise managed to see the poor guy past the ambulancemen and was sure it was Freddie Brown, the garage owner.

At the garage door Lindsay-Joanne had to physically restrain the woman who was desperate to make her way in.

Meantime the body was brought out from beneath the van.

'Best get a stretcher,' the one who had been watching said.

'Hold on a minute,' Denise said.

'What?'

'Why is there blood on the floor where the back of his head was? If he was crushed the back of his head wouldn't be burst open, would it? Crushed maybe but not burst open.'

The medic that pronounced him dead turned Richard's head round. 'You are right.'

'Okay, all of you need to get out. This is now officially a murder scene.'

The mechanic had made his way round the van and stood in front of Denise.

'What's going on?'

'It looks like your boss has been hit on the head then the van dropped on him to make it look like an accident.'

'No way,' he said, then looked out to Freddie's wife who was looking in.

'I will need a statement from you,' Denise said. 'Back at the station.'

'Yes. What now?'

'D.C. Connor will take you all up to the station, we will need to contact headquarters and get a forensic team out.'

Denise ushered the three men out of the garage.

'Lindsay-Joanne, take these men back to the station and get their details, we will need a statement now or at a later date.'

'Billy!' Denise shouted. The ferocity of her call made the men and D.C. jump, added to the fact they hadn't expected her to shout.

'Lindsay-Joanne, tell Billy to park the car and get up here pronto. Oh, have you got a pair of examination gloves, I don't want to leave my prints anywhere.'

The Detective Constable pulled a pair of transparent gloves from her handbag and handed them over, before leaving with the men.

Then she took Mrs. Brown to the side. 'I am afraid it looks like your husband has met with foul play.'

'Foul play? What kind of crap is that?'

'If you want it straight, he is dead. Either as a result of an accident or he has been murdered. Now I need to get more policemen and a forensic squad here, so I think you should go home or to a relative. As soon as we have anything else we will come and tell you.'

'Can I not see him, just for a minute?'

'Mrs. Brown, you could contaminate a crime scene, we might never get the culprit. That's the last thing I want, and I am sure it's the last thing you want.'

Just then an excited younger woman, in her late teens or early twenties, rushed up.

'What is it?'

'It's your father. He's dead.'

As she said it she broke down, the realisation being converted to tears and she almost collapsed into her daughter's arms.

Denise stood watching the sorrowful scene until Billy arrived at the garage front.

'Billy, I am going in to call for back-up, you secure the front door here while I phone from inside the garage.'

Billy nodded. 'Is it Freddie?'

Denise nodded, 'the owner, yes.' She watched the two distraught women slowly leave the garage site before heading back into the garage to phone for help.

In the garage office she picked up the phone and called the Dingwall office. She hadn't a great memory for phone numbers but for some reason that one stuck.

She dialled and quickly relayed the details of the death and requested the help she needed.

On the blotter next to the phone there were a lot of names and numbers. One was circled in red- Jim Rembrandt.

Before leaving she looked around the office but there was nothing out of place, nothing missing. She was sure it wasn't a robbery. What else could it be, she wondered.

Billy stood with his back to the garage door as Denise opened it. Over his shoulder she could see a lot of rubberneckers had gathered.

'Billy, go and get that lot to move back. We need room for the forensics to get in. Any backchat about not moving and tell them they will get arrested.'

'Does it look bad in there?' he asked.

'No. His body was crushed when the van dropped on him, but I reckon he was dead before that.'

'You mean they made it look like an accident.' Wheew, he whistled.

'Right, get the crowd moving. Then I have something I need to ask you.'

The crowd dispersed and quickly formed across the road, jostling for the best viewing position as they did so.

Pleased with his effort Billy walked back up to join his boss.

'So, what do you want to know?' he asked.

'Jim Rembrandt. Who is he?'

'Jim. He and his brother are painters and decorators. Somebody joked once that his painting was better than Rembrandt and he decided to change his business name. Have you not seen their van?'

'Can't say that I have.'

'It says Jim Rembrandt and Johnny van Gogh, master painters.'

'Well, I will need to have a word with him.'

'Why?'

'His name was ringed in red ink on the office blotter.'

'What for?'

'Billy, that's why I need to talk to him.'

'Right.'

Nearly half an hour later Detective Inspector Morton arrived. Before he even got out of the cop car Denise felt her skin crawl.

Morton and his assistant walked quickly toward the garage.

'Denise, how's my favourite Detective Sergeant?'

'I don't know, you will need to ask him,' she said, looking at his assistant.

'So, what do we have?'

'Garage owner, Freddie Brown, found trapped under a van. However, he has a wound on the back of his head which is not consistent with what happened.'

'Thee Freddie Brown that was interviewed by us recently. Okay, let's have a quick look before the forensics guys close the place. Have you any gloves?'

'No.'

Morton looked at her as if she had failed some kind of test.

'I am off duty today. I was passing when I saw the ambulance.'

'Carson,' he said. His assistant thrust a pair of disposable gloves into his hand on command.

With that they all walked in to see the lifeless body of Freddie Brown stretched out on the garage floor.

Morton took the lead and marched in, only stopping when he reached the stiff. He leaned down and looked at the injuries to then moved the head to see the wound.

'Yes, looks like blunt force trauma. He was probably dead

before the van was dropped on his chest.'

Denise felt like saying- no shit Sherlock but said nothing.

'Forensics are here!' Billy shouted in from the garage entrance.

'Okay, let's get out of here,' Morton said. Denise was already heading out before he spoke.

CONNED

DENISE HEADED back into the police station. D.C. Connor had the kettle on, Billy was bringing the panda car back up.

'So, how was your date?' Lindsay-Joanne asked.

'What date?' Denise replied. It was funny that the events of the day had made her forget about the devious Doctor and his deceitfulness.

'You leave the town on a bus. Dolled up to the nines. You received a mystery call from a doctor a few weeks ago. Now, either you were going for a medical appointment or on a date.'

Denise opened her mouth slowly to talk but was too slow.

'Then you arrive back in town the next morning wearing the same clothes. Seems like you had a great night.'

'You could say that. Great night, shit morning.'

'Yeah, well nobody likes walking into a possible murder scene.'

'No, not that.' She looked round to check Billy wasn't about to barge in. 'We had a great night, booked a room then this morning I found out he is engaged to get married in a few months.'

'God, no. You must have been gutted.'

The office door opened, and Billy walked in.

'Kettle's just boiled Billy,' Lindsay-Joanne said.

'Good, I'm desperate for a cuppa.'

'So, what happens now?' Lindsay-Joanne asked Denise.

'We write up our reports and hand them to Morton. He will be taking over the case,' Denise said.

'Not what I was asking about.'

'Not for now,' she replied.

The office door opened again and sleezeball Morton and his assistant walked in.

'Detective Sergeant Kelly, we will be setting up a mobile station at the garage. I want you on my team for this investigation.'

'Sorry, can't help. I am on shifts here.'

'Sorted. I spoke to the chief; your replacement will be starting tomorrow. Welcome aboard.'

Denise managed a false smile. At least the investigation would be interesting.

When Morton and his sidekick and Billy finished for the day Lindsay-Joanne headed through to the back office where Denise was writing up her report of the day's events.

'What were you going to tell me earlier?' she asked.

'When I finish this report I will come through and tell you,' Denise said sharply. 'I hope your reports are up to date for tomorrow morning.'

'They are,' L-J said, disappointed at her boss's attitude as she walked back through to the front office with her head down.

Half an hour Denise came back through.

'Where are your reports?' Denise snapped.

The Detective Constable pointed to the paperwork she had placed on the counter.

'Anything you think might be important to the case?'

'The mechanic who got the van up off Freddie was sent off

on a wild goose chase leaving his boss alone in the garage.'

'Sounds like somebody who knew how they worked in the garage on a Saturday morning. I would expect it to be a local, this backs it up. Well done. Is the kettle warm?'

'No.'

'Well boil it and I'll tell you all about last night.'

Lindsay-Joanne smiled as she hit the button on the kettle.

Lindsay-Joanne sat wide-eyes as she listened to her boss recall of the night before. She certainly looked at her in a different light as she left no detail secret. She almost wished she had been there instead of Denise. The story finished when she got off the bus in Glenfurny and straight into a murder.

'What do you do now?' Lindsay-Joanne asked.

'What, do you think I am so shallow I would be looking for revenge?' Denise asked.

'No, I never thought that.'

'Well, you should have, because he isn't getting away with it.'

Denise lifted her nearly empty teacup and L-J clinked hers in a toast.

'What will you do?'

'That I don't know yet,' Denise said. 'I need to think of something good, so any suggestions welcomed. Although just between us.'

THE CIRCUS ARRIVES

DENISE WAS in the office next morning just after 7 o'clock. Kettle boiling, she was ready for a long day with the incident squad. Just as the kettle clicked the front door opened and Billy appeared.

'You are early,' Denise said.

'Couldn't sleep thinking about poor Freddie Brown. Murdered in his workplace. I mean you don't expect that sort of thing to happen in Glenfurny.'

Denise smiled. Since she arrived less than a year before there had been a murder, an attempted murder, a suicide and a serious sexual assault. Not to mention her predecessor killing himself in the search for the ultimate sexual pleasure.

'You know we are off the case. Well, the station is, I have been seconded to the incident squad. You will be getting a new boss today.'

'Yes I know, we need to show him we are more than competent as a station.'

Denise smiled again. Billy had been a bit shy and reserved when she arrived, but she could see him changing for the better under her guidance.

'I don't doubt you will. Hope you don't mind if I nip up for a cuppa now and then. Don't expect the catering will be as good as here.'

'If you do you will need to bring the biscuits, chocolate, not plain ones,' he said laughing.

Just after nine o'clock the police circus started to arrive in town. Denise had received a phone call telling her to join the other dozen uniforms and detectives outside the garage at nine.

She watched the others arrive in dribs and drabs from half past eight onwards and stood in their own cliques. She headed down just before nine, she didn't need or want to make small talk with a lot of strangers.

Dead on nine o'clock Detective Inspector Morton walked into the group. He did a quick headcount before starting to give out his orders.

'Okay folks, we all know why we are here. There could well be a murderer here in the village. The postmortem later today will either confirm or deny it, until then we treat it as murder. Now,' he said as he pointed to eight officers,' this team will concentrate on door-to -door inquiries. Make sure every house in the street is covered and everyone in each household is spoken to.'

There was a bit of nodding.

'Okay, sort yourselves out in pairs and work out how you are divvying the street up. The other three come with me.'

Densie was one of the chosen three. She hoped Morton wasn't taking her as his assistant. As they walked away from the main group she crossed her fingers in hope.

'Right folks, if this turns out to be a murder we need a quick result. In a small village like this the thought of a killer walking amongst them breeds fear as you can imagine. Carson and I will go to the post mortem at ten o'clock. What is your first task, you know the locals, Denise?'

'I want to speak to Jim Rembrandt, the local painter.'

Morton looked at her as if she had lost the plot. 'Come again.'

'The local painter's business is called Jim Rembrandt. His

name was written on Brown's blotter in his office. I would like to know why.'

'Okay, Michelle will team up with you.'

The woman walked over and stuck out a hand. Denise shook it warmly. 'Detective Sergeant Denise Kelly, pleased to meet you.'

'Detective Constable Michelle Fisher,' she replied with a smile.

'My cars up at the station. We can walk up and get it. I will show you a bit of the town.'

The two walked away leaving the rest behind.

Michelle had a very distinctive English accent. 'So, Michelle, what brings you all the way up here?' Denise asked.

'A man. Met Harry, my husband, who was in the Navy based down local to me. Turned out he was from Dingwall. Are you from around here?'

'No. I am from Irvine in Ayrshire, which is about two hundred miles away. Like you, I also came here because of a man, although I was running away from one.'

'Tell me more.'

'I married another cop. Big mistake. We were hardly back from honeymoon, and he was bedding a colleague.'

'Oh, that's a shame.'

'Worked out for the best. I love life up here. Apart from the murders, that is.'

'Yes, but they keep us in a job,' Michelle said laughing.

Denise drove her car, the yellow peril, as she hadn't been given a police car yet. She had looked up the painter's address in the phone book and knew it was across town. His business address must be the same as his house as it was in a council street.

As she drove Denise pointed out the places of interest around town. Michelle looked on in awe as Denise told her of her adventures, or misadventures, since she had arrived in the town.

Arriving at Jim Rembrandt's home address the van wasn't there.

'Come on, his wife will know where he is, we will knock it,' Denise said, getting out of the car.

Michelle got out without saying anything.

Denise took a second look at the address. Jim and Rose Cameron. Could he be John Cameron's son and involved in Freddie Brown's murder.

Before Denise could press the doorbell the door opened.

'Oh, hi Mrs. Cameron, we were looking to speak to your husband. Do you know where he is working this morning?'

'Yes. He is working at the Highland Hydro. They have a big contract there.'

'Right, thanks. By the way, is your husband related to Johnny Cameron that recently died after a car crash?'

'Yes, that was his dad. Very sad it was. He was devastated, still is to be honest.'

'What about Johnny Cameron?' she asked.

'That's his brother.'

'Okay, well as I said we will need to speak to your husband,' Denise said, then excused herself.

Back in the car she turned to Michelle. 'That's more than a coincidence. Freddie Brown dies and the name on his blotter is Jim Rembrandt, who is really Cameron, whose father died, and Brown was under investigation for being responsible for the crash that led to his death. Can't wait to speak to Jim.'

'The Highland Hydro, that's where I got married. Have you

ever been there?' Michelle asked.

'Yes. Stayed there one night,' Densie said, and left it at that.

BACK TO THE HYDRO

DENISE DROVE round the hotel's car parks until she saw the painter's van. After parking next to it they walked round to the reception area to let the staff know they were in the building.

The receptionist was the same one she had handed the room keys the before. The woman took a double take as she tried to place her. Before she could speak Denise produced her warrant card.

'Hi. I am Detective Sergeant Denise Kelly and my associate Detective Constable Michelle Fisher. We are here to interview Jim Cameron, the painter.'

'Right.'

'Can you point me in the right direction.'

'Yes, they are refurbishing the bedrooms upstairs. They are in room twenty-seven. Would you like me to show you?'

'No, it's okay, we are detectives, I am sure we can find the way.'

The two women headed for the lift.

'Do you think she was being nice or trying to be clever?' Michelle asked.

'If she was clever she wouldn't be earning pennies as a receptionist.'

The smell of gloss paint met the detectives when they stepped out of the lift. The door to room twenty-seven was propped open with a paint tin, the paint smell was even stronger there.

In the room were two painters, although really there was only one and a half. At first they thought one was a dwarf in specially made white overalls, when he turned round they saw it was a young boy, probably just out of school.

The older guy carried on regardless, until the lad called him.

'Visitors,' he said, and slowly he turned to face them.

'Jim Cameron?' Denise asked.

'Yes.'

'D.C. Kelly. We would like to speak to you about Freddie Brown.'

Jim put his paintbrush down on the rim of the paint tin and scratched at his head beneath his paint splattered white woollen hat.

'What about him?'

'In private,' she said.

Jim looked at the boy. 'Take a smoke break Sammy.'

The lad took the hint, and he also put his brush down. As he walked past Michelle she gave him a word of advice.

'Smoking's bad for you, it stunts your growth,' she warned him.

The boy walked past her without even acknowledging her.

'What relationship did you have with Freddie Brown?' Denise asked.

'I have had the van fixed at his garage, that's about it.'

'Your name was written on the blotter in his office.'

Jim shrugged. 'Maybe they wanted painting done. My wife does all that side of the business.'

'I take it you knew he was being investigated with regards to your father's accident,' Denise said, getting straight to the point.

Jim shrugged. 'I just thought it was an accident.'

'Your brother didn't think that. Did he not tell you?'

Jim shrugged again. 'Never mentioned it.'

'Where is your brother? I thought you worked together.'

'He is on holiday for two or three weeks. Driving round Scotland in his campervan. Last he phoned me he was in Edinburgh on Friday.'

Denise knew she wasn't getting anything else from him, so went fishing. 'This looks like a good number, are you doing all the rooms?'

Jim smiled. 'Yeah, one room at a time. When John is here we manage to do two at once.'

'Good money?', she asked.

He just smiled and nodded.

'Perks. Do you get discounts, free food you know, cheap meals?'

'We get leftovers, my mate's wife works in the kitchen, you know. They also said we can get discount on rooms, but it's not something we would usually do.'

'Okay, well when John calls you again tell him I was looking for him and when he comes back from his touring to call in at the police station.'

Jim nodded.

Denise and Michelle headed back towards the car. When they were outside Michelle laughed.

'What's funny?' Denise asked.

'Well, if the brothers are Rembrandt and Van Gogh, who is the midget, Toulouse-Lautrec?'

Denise laughed along with her. 'He isn't a midget, just a

small boy.'

Back in the car Denise put the key in the ignition, but didn't turn the ignition on.

'What's wrong, won't it start?' Michelle asked.

'No. It was something Jim said. It not something we usually do. What do you think that means?'

Before Michelle could think about it Denise was opening the car door. 'Wait here,' she said as she made her exit.

The same receptionist was still behind the main desk.

'Is everything okay?' she asked Denise.

'I don't know. Could you check and see if you had a John Cameron staying here on Friday night?'

The receptionist smiled. 'You mean the painter, yes. Said it was his wedding anniversary, and he was treating his wife.'

'Thanks. Somebody might need to talk to you later and take a statement from you. Thanks for your help.'

Denise walked away. 'Edinburgh, indeed.'

BACK TO BASE

ARRIVING BACK at Glenfurny as Denise headed back to the police station she was amazed to find a mobile incident unit had materialised on the forecourt of Brown's garage.

She slowed as she passed and saw there were still technicians sorting the electrics and other utilities, so she carried on up to her police station. There was space in the car park, so she parked the yellow peril there.

Lindsay-Joanne Connor was alone in the front office when they walked in.

'Lindsay-Joanne, this is Michelle Fisher, she is also a D.C.,' Denise said by way of introduction. The two women simply nodded to each other.

'Kettle ready?'

'What's wrong with the catering van?' L-J asked.

Denise saw it as she drove past. The thought of using it gave her the boak. She never trusted the food from catering vans, the caterers all looked too dirty to be cooking food.

'Never mind that, get the kettle on.'

L-J laughed as she did as she was told.

'Where is the new D.I.?' Denise asked.

'Through the back office. We have only to get him if we need him.'

'What's he like?'

'He is old. Smells of embrocation, or maybe it's embalming fluid. He has terrible dandruff and wears thick rimmed glasses. At least the heat rub masks the smell from his breath.'

'Quite a catch then. Have you asked him out yet?' Denise teased.

'No, I was leaving him for you, seeing as your Doctor didn't work out.'

As they sat at their tea Billy walked in with Susan, the cadet. He was eating his way through a large greasy looking burger.

'Where did you get that?' Denise said.

'I got it from the catering van. It was free,' he said between chomps.

'That's only for those working on the murder investigation,' she said.

'Didn't ask so I didn't say,' Billy said with a shrug of his shoulders and a smile on his face.

'Honestly Billy, you are incorrigible' Denise said.

Halfway through tea the blether and laughing was raised a lot. It was stopped when at a break in the noise there was a loud throat clearing noise. Everyone looked round to see the D.I. who was temporarily in charge of the station looking down his nose at them all, particularly at Denise and Michelle.

'I take it you are part of the investigation based down the road,' he said haughtily.

Denise would have liked to have a bit of attitude, saying this was her station but the Inspector was still her superior. 'Yes sir,' she said. 'I was just asking Lindsay-Joanne about one of the interviews yesterday.'

'And you need to drink tea to ask.'

'No, sir, but Lindsay-Joanne makes the best tea in the town.'

'Really, I wouldn't know.'

'Would you like a cup sir?' Lindsay-Joanne asked.

'No, I never drink the stuff.'

Uncontrollably everybody burst out laughing. Except D.I. McNab who went bright red in the face then turned and disappeared back into the back office.

When the laughing subsided Denise got up and put her jacket back on. 'We better go. Good luck with getting back on his good side.'

'It's okay,' Billy said, 'I will get him a burger from the catering van.'

Denise shook her head as she headed for the door. 'Better check he isn't a vegetarian.'

As she was walking through the front door she heard Billy ask the others what a vegetarian was.

When Densie walked into the incident unit caravan the receptionist called her over.

'Morton's phoned, he said he was correct, blunt force trauma to the back of the head, he was dead when the van landed on him, officially it is now a murder investigation.'

Denise smiled. Not because that she was right, but because Morton took the credit for it, which didn't surprise her.

'Right, we need to interview Terry Jones. He was the guy who found Freddie Brown under the van,' she said to Michelle.

'Who is he?'

'One of the mechanics at the garage.'

The receptionist overheard her. 'The staff were all here earlier asking when the garage would be open. When I told them it could be weeks they decided to decamp to the pub.'

'Okay, we will go there,' Denise said.

'How do you know which pub they will be in?' Michelle

asked.

'What pub? There is only one. The Pheasant Plucker,' Denise answered as she checked her watch. Quarter past eleven, well they will only have been in for fifteen minutes,' she said with tongue firmly in her cheek.

They passed Samson's general store. The shop was busy, open again after the owner's wife was arrested for murdering the owner's pregnant girlfriend.

'I see they do bakery goods. That will make a change from the heavy greasy stuff from the catering van,' Michelle said.

'Sounds like the voice of experience. Are you a regular working with the mobile unit.'

'Yes, well there aren't too many incidents like this one up here in the Highlands.'

'No? I worked a few back in Ayrshire, but obviously none since I moved up here.'

'Do you want me to put a word in with the D.I.?' Michelle asked.

'No, you are all right,' Denise said. Sooner Morton was out of her hair and town the better.

'This is it,' Denise said as she opened the front door of the pub and let the heady atmosphere spill out.

She remembered previously walking there and it was like a gunslinger walking into a saloon. Today she didn't get another look.

There were about a dozen drinkers all busy chatting, no doubt Freddie's death the main topic. The occupied tables all had a collection of full and empty glasses, evidence, if any was needed, that the drinkers had been there more than a quarter of an hour.

Denise walked up to the bar. When the barman, owner Fergus Boothroyd caught the newcomers out of the side of his eye, he stopped his conversation with a woman standing at the bar.

'What can I,' he said before realising who was standing in front of him.

Denise folded her arms in front of her. She waited for an explanation.

'Hi, Detective Sergeant. Would you like a drink?' he said, loudly enough for all the punters to hear. The hubbub died down quickly.

She looked at her watch then up at the pub clock. It clicked on to seventeen minutes past eleven.

'What, you don't think I opened before eleven o'clock? No.'

Denise walked over and looked at the amount of glasses that were on each table. She showed what she was looking at by waving a hand over the table.

'Terrible thirsty they all were, waiting out there until I could open.'

There were nods and agreeable sounds from the drinkers.

'Getting a shock like they have had can make you terribly thirsty,' he reiterated.

'Anyway, I am not here for that. This time,' she said, looking round at Fergus. 'I am looking for Terry Jones.'

All eyes turned to the guy sitting in the corner. Denise followed her eyes and recognised him. He looked different dressed casually, without greasy overalls and a cap on.

'We need to interview you about Saturday.'

'Sure,' Terry said, sitting down his almost full pint of lager and starting to stand up.

'You can finish your pint, Terry,' Denise said.

The guy next to him lifted the pint and took a big swig from it. 'It's okay mate, I will treat it nicely.'

Terry joined the two women detectives, and they left the now noiseless pub. As the door closed behind Michelle who brought up the rear, they heard the noise level shoot up again.

'Where are we going?' Terry asked.

'Just up to the mobile unit outside the garage,' Denise said.

'I don't need to go into the garage, do I?' Terry asked agitatedly.

'No. We wouldn't be allowed in anyway,' Denise said, hoping that would calm him. 'Must have been a big shock, finding him like that,' she added.

'What? Yes. Still can't believe it all really happened.'

At the mobile unit Denise checked that the interview room was ready to use, all the electrics set up and so on. When the receptionist said it was they went through.

Michelle put a new cassette in the recorder and started by introducing the three participants.

'Okay Terry, can you talk us through what happened, starting from when you arrived for work,' Denise asked.

'I arrived at eight o'clock, Freddie was in the office. We only had one job, fitting a full set of brakes to a Ford Transit. About half past nine we were having a tea break when the phone rang. It was a breakdown, an old guy had a puncture, but he thought he might need a tow, so Freddie sent me out.'

'Did you know who the driver was?' Denise asked.

'Yes, it was a Mister Tom Smith. Well, that was the name he gave.'

'Where was the breakdown?'

'Freddie said it was halfway between here and Dingwall, he was phoning from Craighouse Farm.'

He stopped, expecting another question from Denise, but

she just nodded, and he continued.

'Anyway, I drove the recovery truck out the Dingwall Road. I got way past halfway and there was no sign of anybody broken down. I drove up to the Craighouse Farmhouse. The farmer's wife came out and said there had been nobody broken down and they hadn't phoned from there.

When I got back to the garage I walked in and saw Freddie beneath the van. I phoned the ambulance then got the trolley jack out to get the van up. The first jack I got was knackered, there was no hydraulic oil in it. The second one was the same and I had to get oil and top it up. I was running about daft because I was worrying about Freddie. I didn't know he was dead until the ambulance guy told me.'

'Were the jacks usually broken?' Denise asked.

'No. I had never known any of them to be like that.'

'So, how long were you away from the garage?'

'About an hour, maybe an hour and a half.'

'As you drove away did you see anybody hanging around, you know, waiting for you to go.'

Terry shook his head. 'The street was very quiet.'

'What about vans? Were there any parked up along the street?'

'Never noticed.'

'Did you know Freddie was interviewed about the car parts that were put in Johnny Cameron's car before it crashed.'

'Yes, but they would have been wasting their time.'

'Why?'

'It was his wife that did all that, ordering the parts for jobs. She was the garage manager; he was just the head mechanic here.'

'She didn't work Saturday's then?'

'No. She finished earlier than us during the week, but she never worked at the weekend.'

Denise paused for a minute, giving Terry a rest.

'Where did she buy the parts for the garage from?' Denise asked.

'She got most of the parts from her fancy man Richard Dolon.'

Densie looked over at Michelle.

'What do you mean fancy man?' Michelle asked.

'Boyfriend, lover, what would you call him?'

'Oh right. Never heard it called fancy man before, must be a Scottish thing,' Michelle said.

'Who does he work for?' Denise cut in again.

'He has his own company, Dolon's car parts. He has a unit in Dingwall.'

'So, what exactly is the relationship between him and Emma?' Denise asked.

'The story is that Freddie caught them at it in their own bed. Threw her out the house. She was still working here and after a week she was back at home.'

Denise wondered what exactly Freddie Brown had told D.I. Morton when he was interviewed about Johnny Cameron's death.

'Is there anything else you think we need to know about Freddie, Emma or anything else connected with the case?'

Terry looked at his hands, then said 'No, nothing.'

'Michelle, have you anything else to ask?'

'No. I'm sure we can find you again if we need to ask you anything else.'

With that Michelle officially ended the interview.

'Right, thanks for that Terry, you can get back to the pub and your mates.'

'No, think I will head home. When do you think we can get back into the garage then?'

Denise shrugged. 'Could be next week or even the week after,' she conceded.

'What are we supposed to do until then?' he asked as he got up.

'I think the pub could be doing a good trade,' Denise said.

MEETING-TIME

DETECTIVE INSPECTOR Morton called a meeting for 14:00 hrs in the mobile unit. The eight detectives were present. There were no uniforms, Morton had already addressed them outside the unit and asked if any of them had anything pertinent to what happened on the Saturday to attend, nobody had.

'Right folks, a few hours ago Freddie Brown's death was described to me as blunt force trauma to the back of his head. Therefore, this is now officially a murder enquiry. What do we all have?'

There was a lot of silence and looking everywhere but at the waiting Inspector. Denise spoke up.

'Sir, we interviewed Jim Cameron whose father died after a car crash where Freddie Brown was implicated in because he repaired the car. He told me his brother was in Edinburgh, but he really was staying on Friday night at the Highland Hydro. His brother is a bit of a hothead.'

She let that sink in before continuing. 'This morning, I interviewed Terry Jones, the mechanic who found Freddie Brown stuck under the van. He told me Freddie wasn't responsible for running the garage, his wife was. She was also responsible for buying all car parts. Add to that she was having an affair with the guy who ran the car parts company.'

Morton was quiet before moving to the whiteboard to write up some facts. The only things written were Freddie's details and the time and place of his death.

'Right, who wanted him dead,' he started. 'The Cameron's

thought he was responsible for their father's death.'

He looked round for any dissenting words. When there were none he continued.

'Who would benefit most, undoubtably his wife. We need to talk to her next.' He looked over at Denise. 'Go and get her,' he ordered her.

UNDER ARREST

DENISE PARKED the squad car she was assigned outside the Brown's house. It was a huge, detached house with white render and black painted doors and windows.

'Not a bad place for a wee garage owner,' Denise said.

'You bet. Looks like it's been built just for them,' Michelle said enviously.

'Yes, let's go and see the woman of the house,' Denise said as she got out the car.

As they walked up the driveway they could hear music coming from the house. At the volume they could hear it inside it must have been thumpingly loud.

'Party?' Denise said.

'Must be celebrating,' Michelle said smiling.

After ringing the bell twice Denise resorted to banging on the front door.

The music dropped a bit followed by a shout of- 'coming.'

Emma Brown looked shocked when she opened the door and saw the two detectives standing in front of her.

'Oh.'

'Good afternoon Mrs. Brown. Celebrating are we?'

'It's my daughter who has the music on,' she said guiltily.

'We would like you to come with us to the station for a little chat.'

'What about?'

'About your husband's death. It is now been classed as a murder inquiry.'

Emma put a shocked look on her face.

'Right, I will need to get dressed.'

Without being asked Denise walked in with Michelle following, to wait for her.

Inside the house was as expected from looking at the outside. The décor and furnishings looked as though no expense had been spared.

The cops watched from the hallway as Emma put the music off at the big stereo system in the lounge before passing them to head upstairs.

'Wonder where the daughter went,' Denise whispered to Michelle, who just raised her eyebrows and didn't reply.

Five minutes later Emma re-appeared dressed to the nines, but all in mourning black now, much different from the pink tracksuit she had been wearing before. The two cops looked at each other without speaking.

'How long will this take?' Emma asked.

'It's hard to tell, but we will inconvenience you as little as possible,' Denise said.

Emma smiled weakly, the smile of a woman in mourning, unaware that Denise was being sarcastic.

THE GRIEVING WIDOW

DENISE WAS joined for the interview by D.I. Morton. She knew he was surprised by her revelation earlier that Freddie's wife ran the garage after interviewing him, she wondered how good or bad his interview technique was.

Denise did the preliminaries for the interview and waited for Morton to start. He paused before saying anything long enough for Denise to wonder if he expected her to start.

'Now Mrs. Brown, although this is only a formal interview you can have your legal representative with you if you so desire,' he said.

Emma made a dismissing look.

'What were your movements on Saturday morning?' the D.I. asked as he started the interview.

'Got up at seven o'clock. Freddie was already up and had made toast and coffee. We sat together until he had to get ready to go to work. When he left I got dressed, did some housework. Left for the shops at about nine o'clock, did the big weekly shop and got back home about ten thirty.

I was just enjoying a coffee when I got a phone call saying something had happened at the garage. Frantically, I drove up there, when I got there I saw you,' she nodded towards Denise.

'Did you know what your husband was working on that morning?' Morton asked.

'Yes. I was in the garage on Friday when Bob Waite booked his van in for a full set of new brakes.'

'You arranged the spares for the job, I take it you don't keep a huge amount of stock in the garage.'

'No. We just keep light bulbs, fan belts and wiper blades, that sort of thing. I phoned and ordered the brake pads Friday morning, and they were being delivered the next morning at nine o'clock.'

'Where do you order the parts you need from?'

'Unless it's a specialist dealer part we get them from Dolon's car parts.'

'They were delivered then?' Morton asked.

'Yes, as far as I know. Freddie would have phoned them if they weren't there when he needed them.'

'Who would have delivered them? Dolon himself?'

'He lives locally, so I suppose so.'

The Detective Inspector paused again.

'You are having an affair with Richard Dolon, is that correct?'

'No.'

'Oh, so the information I have is wrong.'

Emma looked down at her hands. 'I had a fling with him, not an actual affair.'

'Did Freddie know about it?'

'Yes. When he found out about it we stopped.'

'How long ago was this?'

'Look, what has this to do with Freddie's death?' Emma said quite animatedly.

'Jealous husband confronts sleezy guy who was having sex with his wife. Sleezy guy hits hubby and knocks him out. Drops van on him to make it look like an accident. So, if it was five years ago then it would have been history, if it was last week it would have been raw.'

'It wasn't last week. It was actually last month.'

'How much was Freddie insured for?' Nelson probed.

'What?' Emma asked, caught off guard for a minute.

'Was he worth more dead than alive?'

'No, he was the World to me. No amount of money could replace him.'

'Well, Richard Dolon was doing it a month ago.'

'That's out of order!' Emma said angrily.

'Having sex with somebody out of marriage is out of order in my book, yours is obviously different. So, insurance.'

'I don't know. Freddie did all that stuff.'

'Really? You did all the books and paperwork for the garage, but you let him sort the insurance out.'

Emma sat silently.

'Would the house be paid for?' Denise asked, jumping in.

Emma shot her a look. She hadn't expecting her to ask questions. 'Yes. The mortgage company insisted on it when we took the mortgage out.'

'It's okay, we will look into all your finances,' she added.

'When will the garage be able to be opened? My staff all rely on it for their wages.'

'Hasn't kept them out of the pub. Anyway, the earliest you could possibly get it back will be next week,' Denise continued, giving Morton a chance to decide what way to go next.

'Why?'

Densie looked to the D.I., letting him answer.

'Mrs. Brown, I would think the most important thing you would want is that the person who killed your husband is brought to justice. To do our job properly we need to be sure we have all the evidence we can get from the premises,' he said.

'Sorry, you are right.'

'Detective Sergeant Kelly, anything else you want to ask?'

Denise looked Emma straight in the eye. 'Are you having an affair with anybody else just now?'

Emma looked away. 'No. I realised I made a mistake with Richard.'

'Okay, interview terminated', Denise said then switched the recorder off.

NEXT

AS EMMA Brown was being shown out of the mobile unit Richard Dolon was walking towards it.

Denise was watching out the window and saw them say something, or just mouth it, as they passed. She would wager her next months pay that the affair was still going on.

Back at her desk, she watched as Richard was being shown into the interview room. He wasn't the type of guy she thought Emma would go for. She was all about looking perfect, he certainly wasn't.

Morton walked over and spoke to her before they interviewed Mr. Dolon.

'What do you think of the wife?' Morton asked.

'Either lying or just being economical with the truth. She whispered something to Richard as they passed outside,' Denise answered.

'Could she be behind it?'

'She is definitely a suspect in my eyes.'

'Okay, when you finish your tea we will deal with Richard.'

Densie and the Inspector both introduced themselves to Richard Dolon before starting the interview. Denise did the official stuff then waited for Morton to start. She had been quite impressed with him earlier.

'Mister Dolon, or do you prefer me to call you Richard or

anything else.'

'Richard's fine.'

'Richard, Saturday morning your firm had to deliver brake parts to Brown's garage. Was it done.'

'Yes, of course we did. They ordered, we delivered.'

'Was it you who personally delivered it?'

'Yes.'

'Was Freddie there alone?'

'Yes. I dropped them at the open door and shouted in. When he called back I made my getaway.'

'Oh. What, were you scared of a confrontation?'

'No. I had my good shoes on and didn't want oil on the soles.'

Morton looked at Denise but never spoke. Denise knew the look meant he was thought Dolon was lying.

'Freddie never spoke?'

Richard nodded his head.

'For the record please answer.'

'No, he never spoke, but he waved to me.'

'So, he alive defiantly alive then?'

'What? Yes, of course he was. I saw him moving beneath the front of the car.'

'You are having an affair with his wife, is that why you didn't want to hang around?'

Richard was quiet for a moment.

'No, I was having an affair, it's over.'

'When did it finish?'

'Last week.'

'How long was it going on for?'

Richard thought. 'About two months.'

'Why did you stop the affair?'

'It had run its course.'

'Who decided?'

'It was a joint decision.'

'You see the way I see it, Emma said she wanted you two to be together and if Freddie was out of the picture that would solve it. You got Terry out of the garage on a wild goose chase and hit Freddie before pretending it was an accident.'

Richard shook his head.

'For the record,' Morton prompted.

'No. She had another guy on the go, that was why she dumped me.'

'Oh, she dumped you. So, who was the guy?'

'Don't know. My guess is its one of the mechanics.'

'Did Emma ever mention doing anything to Freddie? Getting somebody to harm him.'

'Not specifically.'

'What did she say specifically?'

'We would be in bed, and she would say things like wouldn't it be great if it was just the two of us, stuff like that. She never said about killing him.'

Morton paused before saying, 'Would you have?'

'No way,' he said quickly.

Morton was quiet again for a moment. 'D.S Kelly, have you anything to ask?'

'I take it you heard about the car crash that eventually led to the death of Johnny Cameron.'

Richard went to nod before remembering and saying- 'yes.'

'Did you know the parts you fitted are being blamed for the crash and subsequent death.'

'No way. Who said that?'

'The collision experts at Dingwall police station. They are saying the parts were second hand although supplied as new.'

Richard looked between Denise and Morton a couple of times. 'I want to speak to my lawyer before continuing.'

Morton smiled. 'Sure. We will stop the interview now. If you could report here tomorrow morning with your brief at nine o'clock. Okay.'

'Sure.'

Denise ended the interview and sat on as Richard Dolon got up and left the interview room.

Morton smiled. 'Let's go for a drink. After that display I think you deserve it.'

WHO IS IN THE FRAME?

BEFORE HEADING to the pub, D.I. Morton gathered the detectives round the whiteboard for a debrief.

'So, what is our feeling about the case, who hit Freddie Brown?'

Denise raised a hand. 'Firstly, John Cameron Junior had a grudge against him because of the death of his father in the car crash.'

'Yes,' Morton agreed. 'We need to speak to him asap. Carson, speak to his brother, tell him he needs to head back, or we will get him arrested and brought back here.'

Carson for once looked bemused. Normally he knew what his boss wanted, this time he didn't.

'I don't know where his brother lives,' he said meekly.

Denise piped up- 'It's okay, I can give you the address.'

'Can you not go?' Carson said to Denise, which instantly incurred his boss' wrath.

'Detective Constable, if I wanted the Detective Sergeant to go I would have asked her to go. Now, get the address off her and go where you were asked to.'

There was an embarrassing silence in the room as Carson got up slowly and walked toward D.S. Kelly.

While the embarrassing moment was happening, Denise

had been writing Jim Cammeron's address down on a slip of paper. When Carson walked towards her she offered him the note. He took it without looking and walked out of the unit.

Morton shook his head, as if none of what had happened was his fault, before continuing.

'We also have Richard Dolon. He was having an affair with Brown's wife. The things we might do for love, eh.'

This was still met with silence.

'Anything else?'

Denise looked at Michelle, hoping she would take a hint, which she did.

'Sir, when we went to Emma Dolon's house today, she was acting nothing like the grieving widow you saw earlier. In fact, I think she was glad to see her husband dead.'

Morton nodded vigorously. 'Yes, we discussed Richard Dolon a few seconds ago,' he said condescendingly.

Denise was anger by his comment. 'Sir, don't forget, Richard said he was finished with her, reckoned she had another fancy man.'

'Good point.' He wrote up on the board- mystery lover.

Denise, sitting next to Michelle, patted her knee encouragingly. Michelle accepted the gesture with a smile.

'Of course, sir,' one of the other detectives piped up, 'it could be that it was a disgruntled customer. Could have just been an argument that went too far.'

'Another good point,' Morton said. He wrote on the board- disgruntled customer. 'Right, any more for any more before we head to the pub. First drinks on me,' he said, to ensure the suggestions stopped.

Denise walked into The Pheasant Plucker and saw

straight away the garage crew had vacated the premises. In fact, the pub was quiet save for a few locals and a couple of cops that were even thirstier than Denise and Michelle.

'Get a seat and I will get the drinks,' Denise said.

'But I thought Morton was getting the first drink,' Michelle protested.

'It's okay, he can get the second,' she said with a smile.

'Vodka and coke then,' Michelle asked for.

Denise said nothing as she headed to the bar.

Another barman was behind the bar. Unsurprisingly Fergus was at the end of the bar, talking to another woman.

'Detective, lovely to see you again,' he said waved to her, smiling.

'Two vodka and cokes please,' she said, ignoring him.

The barman got the drinks and put them on the bar counter.

'These are on the house,' Fergus said, smiling again.

'Thank you, but I don't take bribes. I will however take them as an appreciation of the good work we do keeping you and your fine premises safe,' Denise said to him.

She lifted the drinks and looked at him. 'Right now, we have bigger fish to fry, after that you better make sure you keep to the correct opening hours.'

Fergus looked surprised. 'As ever,' he said innocently.

Morton arrived and headed straight to the bar. With him were two other detectives. He ordered them all pints of beer then walked over with another vodka and coke for the women.

He leaned over and eyed them up, one at a time.

'Great work today. I think we make a great team together.'

Morton the cop was back to being Morton the creepy guy you didn't want to be your boss.

'Thanks for the drinks, sir,' Denise said, hoping he would just turn and leave them.

'Yes, thanks,' Michelle added.

'Not too much, we have Dolon and his brief first thing,' he cautioned Denise.

'No, sir, I will be finished after these,' she said.

Luckily for them, Morton then left and stood at the bar.

'He is a creep, isn't he,' Denise whispered.

'Yes, but I am lucky, it's you he likes,' Michelle said with a smile.

'Please, don't make my skin crawl any more than it does,' she said, then they enjoyed a laugh between them.

BRIEF VISIT

NEXT MORNING Dolon arrived on time with his lawyer. They were shown straight into the interview room.

Morton walked over to Denise's desk. She was sitting pretending to be busy, reading the record of Freddy Brown's interview regarding the state of Johnny Cameron's Hillman Hunter. He said he did the work personally and everything was working perfectly when he MOT'd it.

She had to read it three times before memorising it. Normally it would have been once. If she had stuck with two vodka and tonics she could have. Drinking four left her nursing a throb at the front of her head. Tea and paracetamol hadn't touched it.

'Ready to interview Richard Dolon?' he asked.

Denise didn't look up, didn't want to see his seedy eyes studying her body.

'Yes, let's go.'

Dolon and his brief stopped chatting when Denise opened the interview room door. She walked in followed by Morton.

'Good morning Richard. I see you brought your lawyer.'

The lawyer reached a hand up to shake the Inspector's hand.

'David Hair, I am from Drysdale and Drysdale.'

'Detective Inspector Harold Morton,' he reciprocated.

As expected the hand wasn't proffered to Denise. Well, she

wasn't a man.

Denise introduced those present to the recording machine and waited for Morton to start. Before he could the lawyer interrupted.

'I have a prepared statement from my client. After I read it he will answer no comment to any other questions.'

After that he continued.

'My firm has never supplied used parts; all replacement parts are manufacturer supplied. The car crash that caused the death of Mister Cameron must have been caused by the failure of the brake servo unit as he appears to have lost all front brakes. His firm has not supplied Brown's garage with such a unit this year. His order book is available to check anytime.'

The lawyer paused to see what the cops reaction was.

Morton spoke. 'If Mister Dolon has nothing else to say then we should terminate the interview now. Mister Dolon?'

'No, nothing to add.'

Morton looked round to Denise, who terminated the interview.

Dolon and Hair stood up.

'We will send somebody round to your premises soon Mister Dolon. Just so we can eliminate you.' He smiled insincerely at them both as they left.

Dolon and his brief quickly left the room.

'Well, D.C. Kelly. What do you make of that?' he asked her.

'If Brown's garage didn't get the Hunter parts from there, we need to know exactly where they got them.'

'Correct. I think we need another chat with the grieving widow, don't you.'

She nodded.

'Good. You and D.C. Fisher bring her in. You know the way.'

'Yes sir,' she smiled.

There was no sign of life at the Brown home. They checked both front and back and even tried the doors but found them securely locked.

As they headed back to the car the next-door neighbour waved from her window. As they walked toward the neighbour's house her front door opened.

'She has gone away for a few days. Her and her daughter,' she added.

'Did they say where to?' Denise asked.

'No. Normally they all go abroad, but she said she would be back on Monday. Said she hoped the garage would be open by then.'

'Not much chance of that if we don't speak to her first.'

'If she calls me I will tell her you were looking for her.'

'Right. Does she call you often.'

'No. She never has. I don't think she even has my number, I'm ex-directory see, because of the dirty phone calls. There again, you never know, she could call me.'

'Okay then, Thanks.'

They walked slowly back to the car, not speaking as they did so.

'What do you think are the chances of Emma phoning old nosey neighbour?' Denise asked Michelle.

'About as much chance as me winning the pools.'

'Still a chance you think.'

'Not really,' Michelle said. 'You see, I never do the pools.'

Both women laughed as Denise drove off heading for the

mobile unit and Morton, who will not be happy with the news they have for him.

WHERE IS SHE?

DENISE STOPPED the car outside the pub.

'Hare of the dog?' Michelle asked.

'No. Just wondering if any of the garage workers are in there knows where she might have gone.'

'Bit early for the pub to be open. It's not eleven yes.'

'Oh, our innkeeper here has previous for serving drink early. Come on, let's just see.'

Denise rapped on the door three times, a pause then another two.

The door opened a peep and was going to close again, but Denise quickly stuck a foot in the door.

'Morning,' she said as she pushed it open against a resistance. After a few seconds the door ceded, and Denise found herself inside the pub. Michelle followed her in, and they found half a dozen punters drinking.

Denise looked to the bar and saw a stunned looking Fergus looking back.

'Morning folks. Oh, is that eleven o'clock already,' she said.

'Hare of the dog is it?' he asked.

Denise shook her head. Now it was mentioned there was still a bit of a throb from her head.

'You better hope I find out what I want, or I will be reporting you,' she said to him before turning to the punters.

'I am looking for Emma Brown. I have been told she has gone off for a few days. Anyone know where she might have gone?'

There was a silence. For a moment she thought she would have to go through with her threat to report Fergus before somebody spoke up.

'No doubt she will be at her sister's caravan at Black Rock caravan park in Dingwall,' a tall, well-built guy said.

'Do you work with her at the garage?' she asked.

'Yes, I am a mechanic. Her sister lives in Coronation Street. It's the one with silver gates.'

'Thanks,' she said. Michelle headed out with Denise behind her. As she left she turned round and shouted to Fergus- 'last time.' That was all she said as the door closed behind her.

Michelle drove to Dingwall. The mechanic had been correct, they quickly found Emma's sister's house. She confirmed Emma was at her caravan and even gave directions so they could find the caravan quickly.

Denise was impressed as she put the foot down. The only time Denise cautioned Michelle was as they approached the hill where both she and Johnny Cameron had crashed.

They made great time and quickly found the caravan in the park. There was a car parked outside, so she couldn't be far away.

Denise knocked on the caravan door. Emma opened it and had the same look on her face the last time she found her on her doorstep.

'What?' was all she managed to say.

'We need another chat,' Denise said.

'Now? I need a few days away.'

'If it was up to me I would allow you a few days to grieve,' she lied. 'However, my boss is a hard hearted bastard. We need to see you now.'

'Are you going to bring me back. I can't drive, I've had a few drinks.'

'Yes, we will arrange a lift for you,' Denise agreed.

'Okay, wait until I get my shoes and my bag,' Emma said and went back into the caravan, leaving the door open.

A girl appeared at the door. Denise was sure this was her daughter; she had appeared the day Freddie was found under the van.

'This is harassment,' she slurred. 'Why don't you leave us the fuck alone.'

'Just go inside and sober up,' Denise said.

'Sober up. I am not drunk,' she slurred again.

She raised a shaky hand towards Denise. Before she could move Michelle reached over and grabbed her wrist.

'I wouldn't if I were you,' she said in a low, threatening voice.

The girl was shocked by the intervention and pulled her hand away as soon as Michelle relaxed her grip. Just then her mother appeared.

'Julie, get in and behave yourself. When I am away drink some coffee.'

Even before they got in the car Emma was gibbering like a budgie. Yakking about the caravan being her sister's and that she usually holidayed abroad. Before Freddy died they were talking about buying a place in Spain.

Denise signalled with her hands to Michelle not to engage in conversation with Emma, letting her gibber away to herself. The hope was she said something that incriminated herself.

Michelle drove a bit quicker on the way back to Glenfurny, glad to get away from Emma's constant drivel.

Emma was shown into the interview room, accompanied by a W.P.C.

Denise made a beeline for Morton.

'Sir, we have Mrs. Brown. Unfortunately, she is pissed.'

'At this time,' Morton said, looking at his watch. It had just turned noon. 'Where was she, at The Pheasant Plucker?'

Denise looked at him. Did he know about the out of hours drinking there? Was Michelle a snitch, talking about her behind her back and the fact she wouldn't charge the landlord. She would need to watch her, she thought.

'No. She was in a caravan in Dingwall. Emma and her daughter were both pissed.'

Morton shook his head. 'Is she talking?'

'Talking, she never shut up during the whole journey.'

'Good. Right, let's get the interview done.'

'Sir, I think we should get a doctor to check her, say she is competent to be interviewed. If she told us something that implicates her a good brief say she was drunk and get it thrown out. Could jeopardise the whole inquiry.'

'You are right.' Morton said. He got up and spoke to the receptionist.

Denise went to her desk and wrote up her notes for the morning, including finding The Pheasant Plucker being open early, to cover her back.

The receptionist called Morton and said the local Doctor wasn't available, but she managed to get somebody from the local hospital.

A rumble in her belly reminded Denise she hadn't eaten

since eight o'clock that morning. She decided to give food a bye and try the snack van the police had laid on.

Denise was sitting after lunch letting a solid lump of burger remind her why she shouldn't have eaten from the van when the unit door opened, and a familiar face walked in.

Doctor Grant Jameson. Looking gorgeous as ever, but still a six-foot-tall rat. He didn't look round and give Denise the chance to give him a look. She was good at looks and had a special one reserved for him.

D.I. Morton walked over and introduced himself to the medic and showed him where Emma Brown was.

The Doctor went into the interview room and stayed for about five minutes. Exiting, he walked over to Morton and told him his prognosis.

Morton smiled as he shook the Doctor's hand.

Grant Jameson then walked away without looking back.

Look over in his direction, Denise secretly pleaded with him to look over so that she could turn away, ready to show him she was better, she didn't care about him, he was a piece of shit.

After he opened the door to go out he turned and looked right at her. In that instant she knew he had seen her and only pretending not to.

Denise didn't have time to give him a look, she only had a second, so she raised her right hand and gave him the middle finger. 'Prick,' she mouthed, but too late, he had already gone.

'Ready,' Morton asked as he stood over her desk.

'Yes, sir,' she acknowledged.

'This time I want you to take the lead. Good cop, bad cop with you obviously being the good one.' He smiled as he said it, it made Denise cringe.

'More often I have found a woman will open up more to another female,' he added.

'Yes, I have found that often works.'

'Right, let's go.'

EMMA'S SECOND INTERVIEW

ALTHOUGH DENISE was leading the interview she still had to do the business with the recorder. After doing the introductions she stared straight at Emma.

'Emma, we know you are in charge of ordering the spares for the garage. Where did you get the servo unit for Johnny Cameron's Hillman Hunter?' she asked, getting straight to the point.

'From the usual car part supplier.'

'We have checked their order book, and they haven't supplied a servo unit to anybody this year.' Denise had checked with the two cops sent to Dolon's car part office.

Emma looked at Denise as if she had just been poked sharply in the ribs.

'He must have doctored his books then,' she said. She sounded sober, but still looked a bit tipsy.

'Funnily enough, in your records against the supply of the servo unit it says cash. Simply cash, no mention of who the cash was paid to.'

'I think I need my lawyer.'

'Of course you can get a lawyer. We can stop this interview right now and get him in here. He will probably tell you to answer everything as no comment. This just says to us you are guilty. So, before you get legal advice I think it's in your best interest to be straight with us. Who was the cash paid to?'

'You don't understand.'

'Emma, there is a lot to this case we don't understand. If you don't tell us your side of the story we can't understand.'

Emma pulled at her hair and sighed. 'I was having another affair. Still am I suppose, with Andy Carmicheal, one of the mechanics. Anyway, he started supplying car parts. Said his brother worked in Harlfords in Inverness and got a good discount.

Freddie reckoned some of the parts weren't new. After the crash Andy admitted to me they were from scrap cars he stripped.'

'You were putting used car parts from cars that had been scrapped and selling them as new. Why did you not come to us, it's not your fault if you genuinely didn't know. Andy is the one who would have been charged.'

'He told me not to. That was when I saw another side to him, he threatened me with all sorts. Even violence. He grabbed me and shook me; I was really scared of him.'

'What about your husband? He knew nothing about this?'

'No. I would put the parts in the office and just say they had been delivered. He never questioned me.'

'Parts, how long had it been going on?'

'For the past month or so. It depended what parts he said he had available.'

'What about the affair? How long were you having an affair with Andy?'

'Started five weeks ago. He came to me and offered the cheap parts, and we had sex in my car.'

Denise looked at D.I. Morton. She was having two affairs and probably sleeping with her husband at the same time. His only reaction was to stick his horrible tongue out just past his teeth. She was sorry she had looked over; he was probably getting off on the thought.

With the pause, Morton stepped in. 'Emma, do you think Carmicheal killed your husband, or even had anything to do with it?'

Emma was quite for a time. A long time. Denise was about to intervene when she finally spoke.

'Yes. He was under some strange illusion he could walk in and take over from him. At the garage and with me.'

'Did you encourage him in any way?' Nelson continued.

'No. Definitely not. The sex wasn't even that good. The only thing was it was illicit, that made it exciting, but he wasn't good in bed. Or in the car or the garage.'

Denise tried not to imagine any of it. Morton probably did.

'What makes you think he was involved?'

'When the accident happened, I was driving towards the garage when Andy passed me and gave me a thumbs up.'

'That's it?' Denise asked.

'Yes. He has been phoning me and texting since it happened. I haven't been returning his calls. That was why I ran away to the caravan in Dingwall.'

'Is Andy six foot or just over it, well-built and has a tattoo on his left arm of a dragon?' Denise continued.

'Yes, that sounds like him.'

'Well, he told me where you were, at your sister's caravan.'

Suddenly there was a look of absolute terror on Emma's face.

'How did he?' she mumbled to herself.

'Okay, I think that's all we need from you at this time.

Inspector, anything you want to ask?'

'You think Carmicheal will harm you?' Morton asked.

'I don't know what he is after. Possibly. Probably.'

'We will be going out to bring Carmicheal in for questioning now, but I don't know how long we will be able to hold him,' he said.

'Can the cops that take me back to Dingwall bring me back here. I will hide out in a caravan at the caravan park until I know what's happening with Andy.'

D.I. Morton looked at Denise. Offering a taxi service wasn't part of their remit.

'It's ok,' Denise mouthed, before continuing. 'Okay then, she said to Emma, 'let's get you somewhere safe.' She ended the interview and stopped the recording.

A SAFE PLACE

DENISE AND Michelle drove Emma Brown back to the caravan in Dingwall to get her daughter and her belongings. Morton hadn't been happy at first when they walked out of the interview room, he was old school and believed when the police were finished with you it was up to you to find your own way home.

Denise explained about Emma being pissed and the only way she would come to be interviewed was if she was guaranteed a lift back. Denise said her alternative was to arrest her. When she said to him- how would that look, grieving widow arrested he reluctantly agreed she had done the right thing.

Back at the caravan it was clear Emma's daughter had continued drinking. She was spark out on the sofa, dead to the world.

The two detectives agreed it would be better not waking her but carry her bodily and pour her into the back of the cop car. Emma rushed round and hastily grabbed the belongings they needed.

The caravan park was busy as it was early summer, but not sold out and they easily got a caravan. Emma carried her luggage; the cops carried her daughter.

Inside the caravan Denise put a hand on Emma's shoulder. 'Okay, Emma, your statement will be written up then we will bring it down for you to sign it.'

'What about Carmicheal?' she asked, now she was sobering

up.

'I don't know if you heard the messages on the radio. They have a thumbprint on what they think is the murder weapon. All the male garage staff are being fingerprinted.'

'You will let me know about Andy. Please don't tell him where I am.'

'Of course not,' Denise said.

The incident unit was the busiest it had been since the first day. The mechanics were being brought in for fingerprinting. Denise recognised most of them from seeing them about town or in the pub. Richard Dolon was also there. The only person that she hadn't seen was Carmicheal.

Denise was sitting at her desk when there was a disturbance at the front door of the unit.

Andy Carmicheal was being brought in. He appeared drunk and was handcuffed. Being a big strong guy, it took two officers to keep him in control.

'Fucking stop hurting me!' he roared at the cops that were restraining him.

Nelson walked over to him. 'Calm down Mister Carmicheal. We just need to take your fingerprints.'

'Why? Dolon did it.'

'If he did then you won't object to giving your prints then.'

That blew Carmicheal's argument out the window.

'Wait, you might want to set me up.'

'Why? Dolon did it.'

'I want my lawyer.'

'Tell you what, we will take your prints just now and you can go and sober up, then we will talk to you and your lawyer together.'

The D.I. said it in such a reassuring way that the drunk Carmicheal agreed.

Denise, watching from afar was starting to admire Morton. Obviously only as a police officer.

When the prints were taken Andy Carmicheal was formally charged with fraud, for supplying used car parts as brand new. He was then marched up to the Glenfurny police station as there wasn't a cell in the mobile unit.

Denise walked over to Nelson who was talking to the receptionist. 'What's the evidence like?' she asked.

'Clear thumb print in blood on a heavy tyre rod. If it's Carmicheal's print and Freddie Brown's blood we have him,' Nelson said smiling.

'Right, well Michelle is finishing Emma Brown's statement then we will take it to her to sign.'

'You know she will be also be charged with fraud,' Morton said.

'Yes, but not just now.'

'Oh no. That will go upstairs for them to decide. Like you said, not good P.R. to arrest a grieving widow before her murdered husband is even planted.'

'What about Carmicheal, when will we interview him?'

'Oh, I think he can cool his heels tonight and we will talk to him tomorrow morning.'

'Okay sir. Sounds like a good idea.'

'Are you joining us for a drink tonight?' Morton asked.

He looked at her like a big cat surveying his prey. She imagined he would like to get her drunk and take advantage of her. That, she was certain, would never happen.

'Not tonight sir. Washing and ironing needed.'

'If you change your mind you know where we will be.'

With that thought on her mind she headed over to see if Michelle was nearly finished her typing.

MORNING ANDY

DENISE LOOKED up from her desk and saw Andy Carmicheal being led into the unit and straight into the interview room. A few minutes later his brief, local lawyer Gary Anderson, walked in and joined him.

Morton walked over and put his head round the interview room door and had words with them. Straight afterwards he walked over to speak to Denise.

'They are asking for fifteen minutes to confer,' he told her.

'I take it you are the lead this time,' she asked, although she knew the answer.

'Yes,' was all he said before walking away.

Carmicheal's brief put his head round the interview room and signalled to the D.I. they were ready. Morton got up and signalled Denise to follow him.

Inside the room Denise set up the recorder and introduced everybody in the room, then waited on Morton.

'Mister Carmicheal, did you supply second hand parts to Brown's garage and say they were new parts?'

Andy looked at his brief, who obviously signalled something silently. 'Yes. But, I must add they were as good as, if not better than new,' he answered.

'Well for your information we obtained a warrant and removed a large number of spare parts from your garage. These are currently being examined at the police garage in Dingwall.'

Carmicheal turned to his lawyer. 'Can they do that?'

Anderson nodded. 'If they obtained a warrant, yes.'

'Well, anyway those are for my own use.'

'What kind of car do you own Mister Carmicheal because there were parts for everything from a Hillman Hunter to a Transit diesel van.'

'I sort cars on the side.'

'Well, if you are putting used spares in the cars you repair, and they are not fit for purpose then that is just the same as you did with the parts that went into Johnny Cameron's car.'

Carmicheal didn't speak and Morton let that hang in the air for a moment.

Andy Carmicheal looked at his brief who looked back without indicating anything.

'Emma Brown had told us you and she were having an affair, is that correct?'

Carmicheal nodded.

'Please answer for the tape,' Denise intervened.

'Yes. Well, we had sex twice, if you call that an affair.'

'Did Freddie know?' Morton continued the questioning.

'Only if she told him. I kept shtum.'

'You aren't currently married, are you?'

'No. I am single, split up with my partner a few months back.'

'That was when she ran away from you to a woman's refuge in Dingwall,' Denise intervened, being the bad cop.

Carmicheal turned quickly and looked at her as if he wanted to slap her. 'That was only so she could get a flat there in Dingwall.'

'That's not what the medical report said,' she continued.

'Did you think that when Freddie was out of the scene you would fill his boots? Morton asked.

'What? No. I suppose it could have been a possibility; you know, when things died down a bit.'

'Did Emma ask you to do it?'

'No.'

'Didn't even suggest it?'

'No.'

'Were you at the garage on Saturday morning?'

Carmicheal looked over at his brief again before answering.

'Yes. I went in and borrowed a couple of tools I needed for a job I was doing on a homer.'

'Freddie was there?'

'Yes.'

'Alone?'

'Yes.'

'Did you or Emma phone the garage and pretend you had broken down to get Terry Jones out of the way, leaving Freddie alone? Did you know there was only the two of them working that morning?'

'Yes,' Andy said, then realised the detective had asked two questions at once.

'I mean yes, I knew it was only Freddie and Terry in the garage that morning. I did not try to get Freddie alone, it just so happened he was when I got there.'

Morton looked at Denise. He was doing so to signal he knew Andy was lying.

'Lovely big house she owns,' Denise said. 'It would be good to own half of the garage instead of grafting for somebody else.'

Andy looked at her. But said nothing.

'Did Emma offer you half the business? The thing is, she is setting you up for the lot,' Denise said, fishing without a line.

'Setting me up?'

'Yes. Says you got the spare parts from your brother who works in Halfords. Didn't know they were from scrap cars.'

'Lying bitch,' he spat out.

'So, are you saying Emma knew the parts weren't new?'

'Yes, she knew.'

Gary Anderson, Carmicheal's brief tugged at the sleeve of his jacket.

'What were you doing with the money you were skimming from the parts?'

'It was only that one time,' Andy said.

Morton shook his head. 'Not what Emma said,' he said.

'Then she is lying.'

'Detectives, I think we should have a little recess now so that I can speak to my client,' Gary Anderson announced.

'Interview paused at nine-twenty-five,' Denise said, then the two cops got up and left the room.

'I think he may confess,' Morton said when they were far enough away from the interview room.'

'Bet you a pint he doesn't confess during the next part of the interview,' Denise said.

'Going for a drink tonight, are we?' Morton asked with a smile.

'Only if I have to buy you a pint, which I won't.'

INTERVIEW CONTINUED

TEN MINUTES later they were back in the interview room. The brief had his notepad on the table, Morton thought he was going to read a statement out. The pint would be his- he was wrong. Andy and his brief sat waiting for the next question.

Disappointed, Morton started the questioning. 'Have you had time to think about your answer to that last question. How many times have you sold or fitted used parts that you claimed were new?'

'Between ten and twenty times.'

'Making you what, a couple of hundred quid?'

'Yeah, something like that.'

'You could be doing jail time for a couple of hundred pounds.'

The look on Andy Carmicheal's face told how surprised he was by Morton's claim. He looked at Gary Anderson. His face wasn't denying it.

'Is this a set up?' he asked Morton.

'No. The thing is Johnny Cameron died of a consequence of the faulty part you supplied to Brown's garage. It was found on the post mortem that he died due to a blood clot caused by the compression of his legs in the car crash.'

Carmicheal hid his face with his hands.

'What exactly would you say your current relationship is with Emma Brown?' Denise asked.

When Carmicheal pulled his hands down he now looked puzzled. 'We covered this earlier.'

'You said you had sex twice and that was it. Why then have you been constantly calling her and messaging her to call you?' she continued.

'Who told you that?'

'She did.'

Carmicheal looked at her as if she was making it up.

'I've seen her phone record,' she continued, lying, poking a stick at the wounded bear.

'Bollocks.'

'She told me you killed Freddie and wanted to be with her.'

'Fucking bitch,' he said, raging at her,

Carmicheal's brief then pulled at his sleeve to stop him, but he had lost it.

'We made a pact to kill him, make it look like an accident, but she has fucked it!' Andy Carmicheal said loudly.

'Sorry, Andy,' Denise said, 'looks like you have fucked it.' Denise said, trying to hide the joy in her voice.

JUST ANOTHER MONDAY

AFTER ANOTHER week on the case Denise was excused, the mobile unit removed, and the garage was set to be opened again.

Andy Carmicheal had been charged with murder of Freddie Brown; the murder weapon had his fingerprint on it in blood. He was also charged with fraud for supplying used car parts as new.

On the Monday morning Denise was back behind the counter at Glenfurny police station. Just as the kettle boiled she was joined by D.C. Lindsay-Joanne Connor.

'Oh, you are back,' Lindsay-Joanne said, surprised.

'What, did you think it would take me longer than to solve a murder inquiry?' Denise said.

'No,' she simply said.

'Tea?' Denise asked.

'Yes,' L-J said meekly.

They sat drinking their tea quietly. Denise started the conversation. 'This was your weekend off, wasn't it?'

After she said it she wasn't sure. Her new D.I. might not have agreed with Denise's methods and shift pattern.

'Yes,' was all she replied.

They continued drinking their tea in silence. Finished her brew, Denise wanted to know what was going on or had been.

'So, what do you have to tell me?' Denise asked.

Lindsay-Joanne looked at her guiltily.

'You won't be happy.'

'Lindsay-Joanne, my life is so shit nothing you could tell me would make me even more unhappy.'

Lindsay-Joanne looked at the floor. 'I slept with him.'

'Who? Not Billy,' she said. She couldn't think of any males they both knew. Then an even more horrifying thought hit her. 'Wait, not Detective Inspector McNab.'

'Oh God, no. No, I mean the Doctor.'

'The Doctor. You mean Grant Jameson. You slept with Grant Jameson after what I told you.'

'It was because of what you told me. God, I hadn't had sex for months. When he was needed at the incident unit he turned up here by mistake. One look at him and I understood why you fell for him. He phoned at the station later in the week and asked me out. You were right, he was good. No, he was brilliant.'

Denise didn't know whether to be angry or jealous.

'He told me when he phoned he was single. So, when you are getting your revenge I will be standing next to you, even though I knew the truth.'

Denise was still swithering about how she felt.

'Look, if you hate me I will ask for a move.' As she said it tears welled in her eyes.'

'Come here,' Denise said, getting up and hugging her. 'Lindsay-Joanne, don't be stupid. After seeing him I don't blame you. The only problem is he is a shit.'

The two laughed and Denise kissed her gently on the top of her head.

'Have you two gone funny?' Susan Maxwell said as she walked at that very moment.

'What are you talking about?' Denise asked.

'Cuddling and kissing each other.'

The two laughed again. 'No, more like a mutual appreciation,' Denise said as they broke up.

'Well, I don't want to join in.'

'Come on in, the kettle will need boiled again.'

'No, it's okay, I have juice with me.'

'Juice, have you gone funny?' Lindsay-Joanne said, this time they all laughed.

The phone rang just after ten o'clock. Susan and Lindsay-Joanne were out on the beat. Lindsay-Joanne didn't usually go out walking, but it was a nice day, nothing was happening and although Denise and her were getting on okay she needed a bit of space. That left Denise alone in the front office. She wasn't in the back office as it still smelled of deep heat, an unwanted present left from D.S. McNab.

'Glenfurny police station,' was all Denise got out before the caller spoke.

'One of my neighbours is spying on me.'

'How do you mean spying?'

'Looking in my windows after dark. I have got evidence.'

'Okay, what's your name?'

'Caroline. Caroline Baker.'

'And your address.'

'42 Dingwall Drive.'

'Will you be in all morning?' She said she would be. 'Right, as soon as I get the team together I will be over.'

Denise got in the panda car and drove round town looking

for the other two women. After 15 minutes going round where she thought they might be it dawned on her where they would be, the public park.

It was the start of the school holidays, and the park was alive with kids and their parents. Plus, two skiving policewomen.

The car park was full, so Denise parked the car on the roadway outside it and blasted the horn. Just once was enough and Lindsay-Joanne and Susan hurried over.

'What's up?' Lindsay-Joanne said as she got in the passenger seat.

Denise waited until Susan was in the back of the car before telling them.

'A woman phoned in said she has a peeping tom spying on her.'

'Is that all?' Susan said.

'Susan, do you never read up on crime statistics?' Denise said, angry at the cadet's reaction. 'Most sexual assaults are carried out by men who start out watching, then it turns to stalking then the build up the courage, although that might not be the best word to describe it, then they attack.'

'Sorry, I didn't know.'

'When D.I. Morton was looking at you didn't it make your skin crawl?'

'It did a bit.'

'Then imagine there was somebody in the bushes at your aunt's house spying on you. Watching to see if you get undressed, imagining what he would do to you if he met you in the woods as you were walking home in the dark.'

Susan was silent.

'Not a nice thought, is it?'

'No.'

'Well, there is some guy out there doing that to Caroline Baker and it's our job to find him before he gets any further with his fantasies.'

A FAMILIAR FACE?

DENISE PARKED the car directly outside number forty-two. The curtains twitched in the house; she was obviously waiting patiently for them. Denise was sure a few other curtains were being twitched, hopefully if he was a neighbour the culprit would see they were onto him.

The front door opened before Denise got to knock it. Inside the house stood a tall, blond, gorgeous looking woman.

'You look familiar, are you a nurse?' Denise asked.

'Yes.'

'You were at the car smash between here and Dingwall.'

'That's right. I recognise you now.'

'The old man died; I take it you heard.'

'Yes. Such a shame.'

'Now, about this person that's been spying on you.'

'You better come in.'

All three walked in and joined Caroline sitting in the living room.

'I wasn't going to bother you, but I live here on my own since my mother died two years ago.'

'No, it's important these things are nipped in the bud. Could lead to something more sinister,' Denise said. 'You said you had proof.'

'Yes. Out the back door.' She got up and headed through the

house, with all three detectives following.

Beneath the kitchen window was a flower bed in which were two big footprints. Caroline pointed to the window. 'The windows were cleaned yesterday, but you can clearly see two nose prints on it.'

'Couldn't be much clearer,' Denise said. 'Okay, Susan, stand in the footprints and put your nose against the window as if you were looking in.'

'Don't you want to take plaster casts of those,' Caroline said before Susan could move forward.

'Not at this stage,' Denise said, and Susan did as directed. Her nose hit the glass a good six inches above the other two prints.'

'What height are you?' Denise asked the cadet.

'Six-foot one inch,' she said.

'I reckon we are looking for somebody about five foot six. Shoe size?'

'Size seven,' Susan replied.

'The footprints are about the same size, but you are wearing police issue shoes, so I reckon he was wearing size eights. So, somebody five-foot six tall wearing size eight shoes. Doesn't give us much to go on, but it's a start.'

Caroline looked disappointed.

'Is there anything else suspicious. Anybody being awkward about you?'

'No.'

'Okay, we will knock on a few doors, see if anybody has seen anybody hanging around. Could be they are getting spied on too, just didn't want to bother us. As I said, we will knock on a few doors, I will let you know if we find anything out.'

'Thanks.'

Denise took Susan with her while Lindsay-Joanne went on her own.

'Okay Susan, I will take the lead for the first couple then you can have a go.'

Susan smiled a bit uneasily.

First door, her neighbour in number forty. It was a guy probably in his sixties. He answered the door in jeans and a string vest. He was very hairy, and the hairs poked through the holes in the vest.

'Good morning sir. Caroline next door said she was having trouble with people sneaking about her back door. Have you noticed anybody?'

'No,' he said gruffly.

'Do you live here alone?'

'Yes, since my wife died. Samantha Fox drops bye when she is in the area, but apart from that I am all alone.'

Denise ingored his poor attempt at humour. 'Okay sir, if you do see anything you can contact us at Glenfurny police station.'

Meantime Lindsay-Joanne was across the road. The neighbours there would have seen anyone sneaking round the side of the house.

Denise and Susan carried on and knocked another three doors, all producing nothing.

'Where would you suggest next?' Denise asked the cadet.

Susan thought for a minute. 'What about the houses that back onto Caroline's property.'

Denise gave her the thumbs up. 'Good thinking. We will make a detective out of you yet.'

'I need to be a policewoman first.'

'Okay, well you are interviewing next.'

The guy that answered the door in the house that backed onto Caroline's place carried the newspaper with him.

'What?' he barked, unhappy at being disturbed.

'Sorry to bother you sir. Your neighbour behind you has reported an intruder.'

'Yes, well he must fucking hate rhubarb, he's jumped over mine.'

With that the old guy threw his paper down and stepped out and walked round the side of the house with the two cops following in his wake.

'If I catch the twat I will kick his baws,' he muttered as he walked in front of the women.

Sure enough, his rhubarb had been flattened, obviously standing on it and climbing the fence was his method of entry to Caroline's back garden.

'You don't know who did this?' Susan asked.

Denise shook her head gently.

'Do I know who did it? The bastard would be in traction if I caught him.'

'Do you know when it was done?' Susan added.

'Last night. I was out yesterday and gave them a foliar feed. Waste of fucking time that.'

Susan looked to Denise. She nodded.

'Okay sir. What I would advise you is if you see anybody in your back yard you should call us immediately.'

The old guy, he was eighty if he was a day, looked at Denise and Susan as if they were daft. 'So, the guy is obviously intruding, as you said, at night. You only work dayshift, so what is the point in phoning you?'

Susan opened her mouth to answer but Denise stepped in.

'If you just waited sir, I was going to give you my card which has both the police station and my personal number on it,' Denise said.

'Oh. Right, sorry.'

Denise opened her handbag and handed him one of her cards. 'You should get me or one of the other officers on one of those numbers.'

The old man took the card and studied it. He went quiet for a minute, then looked at her with teary eyes.

'Denise was my late wife's name,' he said.

'I am sorry. She must have been a lovely woman,' Denise said.

'Thanks,' the old man said.

Denise and Susan left him in the back garden with his memories.

Denise checked with Lindsay-Joanne and reported back to Caroline what they found- very little- then headed back to the cop shop.

As they drove Lindsay-Joanne suddenly made an announcement. 'You know if I was into women, which I am most certainly not, Caroline Baker would be my dream date.'

Denise smiled but said nothing. The thing was, the first time she clapped eyes on Caroline, she felt the same.

'Suppose I would too,' Susan piped up from the back of the car.

'Oh, I will fancy her too then,' Denise said, then all three women laughed.

HE'S BACK

DENISE LAY on her bed getting ready to drop off. She was off the next day and had a lot to do. Domesticity was becoming the norm for her. The phone rang in her living room.

Who could it be? Very few people had her home number. Could be an emergency she guessed and grudgingly got up.

'Hello.'

'He's back.'

Denise tried to sift through the possibilities of who he could be and who was phoning to advise her of the fact.

'The rhubarb trampler,' the called added, then suddenly it all fitted into place. Caroline's peeping tom was back. She had to get there quickly.

'I am on my way,' she said, hanging up the phone and hurrying through to get dressed as quickly as she could.

Instead of heading for Caroline's house, Denise headed to the old guy's house behind Caroline's. Parking up she walked to the back of the house and picked a spot where she could see Caroline's garden. But without being seen herself.

From her hiding place she could see a dark figure at the back of Caroline's house. The kitchen was in darkness, no doubt he was waiting to look in the window. She was sure he would jump back over the fence, trek through the rhubarb and make his way through the garden and away.

He was in for a shock, Denise was waiting for him.

Just as the kitchen light went on a quiet voice spoke behind her.

'Is he still there?' the old guy asked.

Standing in the silence and concentrating on the view in front Denise got the fright of her life. When her heart got back to normal beat she whispered back without looking round.

'Yes. Caroline has just walked into the kitchen.'

The old guy moved beside her and watched.

The peeping tom had hidden and watched Caroline check outside before starting to wash her dishes at the sink. Then he stood at the side of the window watching from an angle.

They could see his hand rub the front of his jogging pants then slip inside.

'Dirty wanker,' the old guy whispered.

'Ssshhh,' Denise hissed back at him. Realising if she was going to handcuff the voyeur she realised she needed both hands free and handed the old guy her large police issue torch. 'Hold this.'

After a few minutes the watcher got more brazen and moved to the middle of the window, staring in as Caroline was no longer standing at the sink.

Suddenly there was a banging noise. Caroline had obviously saw him and rattled the window.

Startled, the guy turned and ran. Heading straight for the neighbour's fence.

As he landed on the rhubarb patch Denise made a grab for him.

'Stop, police!' Denise called. As she grabbed the guys jacket it slipped out of her hand, and he escaped her clutches. Denise wondered why the old guy hadn't switched her torch on to help them see who the perpetrator was up close.

A loud crash and a yell answered it. The torch then lit up the area where the noise came from, and she saw the peeping tom was lying on the ground holding his leg and squealing in pain.

The old guy had moved his garden bench across the pathway he knew where the pervert would run, and the booby trap worked a treat.

Denise got her cuffs ready and yanked his arms out and cuffed them behind his back. As she did so she felt his hands were wet, slimy and realised what was on his fingers.

He had been wanking off and she had the result on her fingers. 'Urgh,' she said, then rubbed her hands dry on his t-shirt.

'What's your name?' she asked him while the house owner shone the torch on him.

'Fuck off!' he replied.

Denise pulled at the cuffs behind his back.

'What the fuck are you doing?' he asked, grimacing at the pain.

Then Denise pulled the cuffs and his arms up, causing him pain and discomfort. 'Let's try again, what is your name?'

'It's Darren North. Stop that.'

'That was easy.' Then she read him the Miranda rights. 'Come on, let's go to the station.'

'What, are we getting the train somewhere?' Darren said.

'Comedian, eh. Well, we will see if a night in the cells cools your sense of humour.'

'Thanks for your help, mister,' it was then she realised she hadn't asked the old gent his name.

'Peabody. Ernest Peabody.'

'Right, thanks again Ernest.'

'Will you manage him okay.'

'Sure. Dealt with wee scroats like him often.'

NICKED

DENISE POPPED Darren North into the first cell in the police station. She checked the spare key wasn't on the window sill then locked him in.

'Can you phone my mum?' Darren said.

Denise shook her head. 'Big man until you get nicked then you want your mum. I need to phone Dingwall first, to get them to take you over there.'

'To Dingwall. Why?'

'To the jail there. You will stay overnight then be charged then go in front of the judge in the morning.'

Darren was babbling on about something, but Denise ignored him and phoned the Dingwall station.'

She explained her situation then was hit with disappointment, not for the first time when she called them. Putting the phone down she turned to Darren and gave him the news.

'Looks like it's just us two in here tonight. There was a rammy at the Ross County game tonight, the cells there are all full.'

'Will you phone my mum.'

'What's the number?'

Mrs. North answered the phone after three rings.

'Mrs. North, it's Detective Sergeant Denise Kelly at Glenfurny police station. Your son has asked me to call you, he has been arrested and will be charged with breach of the peace and criminal damage.'

'Darren. Are you sure it's my wee Darren.'

'Yes, it's your wee Darren.'

'I will kick his arse for him. Where was he doing whatever it was he was doing?'

'In Dingwall Road. He was looking in a young woman's window putting her in some distress.'

'So, what happens now?' Mrs. North asked.

'He will stay here overnight then be charged in the morning. Later he will be transported to Dingwall County Court where he will go in front of the judge.'

'Will he be jailed?'

'Not for this, no.'

'Pity, I could do with a few months peace. Okay, thanks for letting me know.'

'No problem.'

Denise's next call had to be made from the back office, away from listening ears.

'Evening Caroline. Just to let you know the lad that was looking in your window tonight has been arrested.'

'Oh, that's good news.'

'He will be charged tomorrow when the procurator fiscal's office opens then he will be up in front of the judge.'

'Thanks for letting me know. I will sleep easier tonight.'

'One bit of advice I might give you. Either wear clothes walking about the house or close the curtains. You will have every randy sod in the town queuing up to look in your window if you walk about in the nude all the time.'

'Okay,' she said, 'I will close the curtains.'

Denise lit the coal fire in the office and snuggled up in one of the chairs in front of it. She had been there before and managed a half-decent kip.

When Billy arrived for work next morning he was surprised to see Denise there and the kettle boiling.

'Thought you were off today, have you swapped shifts?'

'No. I have been here all night.' She pointed to the cell and Billy noticed a shape beneath the covers on one of the two bunks.

'Who is it?' Billy asked.

'Darren North.'

'What's he done now?'

'Breach of the peace and criminal damage.'

'Strange, he has been behaving for the last two years,' Billy said.

'Why, what did he do before?'

'He was stealing knickers from washing lines.'

Denise shook her head. She was sure he hadn't been behaving for the last two years, only hadn't been reported or caught before the previous night.

'When am I getting my breakfast?' Darren shouted after being wakened from his slumber by their talking.

Denise walked round to the front of the cell. 'This is the police station, not the Ritz. You can have a cup of tea and some biscuits.'

'This is police brutality!' he shouted again.

'The tea isn't that bad, Billy said.

Nine o'clock on the dot and Denise was on the phone to the procurator fiscal's office. She outlined the case, and the evidence then sat and waited for them to phone back.

Ten minutes later she got the call then formally charged Darren. Just as she did so D.C. Lindsay-Joanne walked into the station.

'Oh,' she said, surprised that Denise was there.

'Problem?' she asked.

'Yes, two,' Denise answered. 'Firstly, I have just charged Darren here with a breach and criminal damage. Secondly you are late.'

'Yes, sorry. I slept in.'

Denise shook her head. 'Right, I am heading home for some shut eye. You contact Dingwall and arrange transport for Mister North to the court. Think you can manage that?'

'Yes,' she said meekly.

'Right, I will drop in later, to see if you managed that simple task.' Denise walked out and left them to it.

NOT ALL SURPRISES ARE NICE.

ALL FOUR staff were in the station for the first time since they started working the seven-day shift. The others were getting trained in new Health and Safety rules by Denise who had already completed the course at headquarters in Inverness the week before.

The other three were writing the answers to a test while Denise read through the next section to be ready when the door-bell dinged, indicating a new arrival.

Before turning round Denise heard a voice she thought she'd never hear again.

'Hello dear wife. How are you keeping?'

The hairs on the back of her neck stood up. She turned and looked at him. 'What the fuck are you doing here?' she said loudly.

The others forgot their tests and looked up to watch what was going on.

'I came to see how you are.'

'Long way to come, now you have seen me you can fuck off back to whatever stone you crawled out from under.'

'That's the thing, I haven't come that far. Just from Inverness actually. Transferred up a couple of months like you did. It's Detective Inspector Kelly now.'

'Oh, better rank. What does that mean, you have upgraded from cadets to higher ranks to have affairs with?'

'No. Since you left I haven't been seeing anyone else. I came here to try and make our marriage work. After all, you haven't applied for a divorce yet.'

'Only because you aren't worth wasting any money on.'

'You know I have missed you. So has Cyclops.'

'Well, I haven't missed you. So, you and your Cyclops can fuck off! I mean now, as in right now!'

'Billy, show him off the premises,' Denise ordered.

Billy got up from his chair. But John Kelly already had his hand on the door handle.

'This isn't the end of us,' he said, then left.

Everybody got up and consoled Denise.

'Think we need a tea break,' Denise said and hit the button on the kettle. 'We can get stuck into the tin of Rover Assortment Caroline Baker brought in for getting rid of her voyeur.'

As they waited for it to boil Billy turned to Denise.

'I take it that was your husband,' he said.

Everybody looked at him, then laughed.

'Billy, you can be a right clot sometimes.'

Billy just smiled and nodded.

WEDDING DAY

14 JULY 1973 was a big day for Denise and Lindsay-Joanne, Doctor Grant Jameson's wedding day and they were going. They weren't invited to the ceremony; they were just going to watch.

The wedding itself was at St. Clements church in Dingwall. Denise drove the yellow peril, and they arrived while the service was going on. Struggling out of the car, they struggled to walk to the church as they had to park two streets away.

Arriving at the front of the church they were only another couple of folk waiting on the bridal party to leave after the ceremony.

'He will be surprised to see us.' Lindsay-Joanne chuckled.

'Yes, especially like this,' Denise answered.

A quarter of an hour later the front doors opened and a few seconds later the good Doctor and his new wife stood at the top of the church steps and looked out at the twenty or so folk that had now gathered, waiting for them to appear.

Grant was all smiles until he saw the two detectives who were waving at him. The look on his face was priceless as they were both done up to look pregnant. What made it worse was that they looked authentic.

They watched him grit his teeth then try to ignore them.

'Revenge is sweet,' Denise whispered to Lindsay-Joanne.

'Yes, just a pity he was so good in bed. She is a lucky girl,' L-J replied.

Just at that the new Mrs. Jameson noticed the two pregnant looking women. She nudged Grant and whispered something.

They watched him try to placate her, but the women could tell she wasn't satisfied with his answer.

As they were about to leave the other the other guests who left from side entrances spilled out around them. Turning round Denise came face to face with Chief Inspector McKenzie, who looked as surprised to see her looking pregnant as she was to see him there.

The Chief Inspector had been a mentor to her since she arrived in the Highlands. God knows what he would think of seeing her suddenly eight months pregnant. She hadn't been pregnant the last time she saw him a couple of months before.

Denise smiled at him then grabbed Lindsay-Joanne's hand and led her quickly away.

'Quick, we need to get away quick.'

'Why?'

'I just saw the Chief Inspector and he recognised me. I expect I will get a phone call on Monday morning.'

That night, as they were both off for the weekend, the two detectives decided to head to the pub. The Pheasant Plucker wasn't anything to rave about, but it was handy for walking home, especially when drunk, which was their plan.

Denise opened the pub door first and walked in with Lindsay-Joanne walking behind her. They had scoffed a bottle of white wine back at Denise's gaff before heading out, so they were in good spirits.

Denise walked up to the bar with her subordinate trailing behind her. 'What do you want?' she asked.

'A good shag,' L-J whispered, 'plenty guys here, there must be a fit one.'

She was right, the place was packed, some couples but it was mostly men.

'What do you want to drink, dummy,'

'Vodka and coke, with a big coke,' she said, giggling.

The barmaid walked over.

'Two vodka and cokes,' Denise ordered.

'I'll get these,' a voice said over her shoulder.

'What the fuck are you doing here,' she said without looking round. She caught a glimpse of her husband's smiling face in the mirror behind the optics in the bar and felt a shiver run down her back. He literally now made her skin crawl.

'I am on a break at the caravan park in town. Nice place.'

'They have a bar down there.'

'Yes, but you aren't in it.'

'We might go there after this drink; the atmosphere will be better than in here.'

Denise looked in the mirror and saw he had moved away.

'Are you okay?' Lindsay-Joanne asked her.

'Yeah. I just wonder what he is after.'

'Looks to me like it's you.'

'Yeah, well that will never happen.'

They got their drinks and looked round for a seat. Luckily there was a couple leaving and they squeezed in next to another group of girls.

'He is actually good looking,' Lindsay-Joanne said, looking over at him.

John Kelly was standing with a group of guys who looked like other cops. Every now and then he glimpsed over. Denise ignored him but her colleague had been sneaking looks at him.

Denise looked at her. 'I hope you are not thinking what I am thinking.'

'What? No. Not when you told me what a shit he is. I just meant you have good taste. Well, in the looks department.'

Then she leaned in secretly, 'was he good in bed?' she asked, giggling again.

Denise leaned in to answer. 'I thought he was until I slept with the good Doctor.'

They laughed again.

'Come on, drink these up then we can go elsewhere. Knowing he is under the same roof as me makes my skin crawl. Has he been looking over?' Denise asked.

'Yes, but I think he is wondering who the gorgeous woman you are hanging about with.'

'Shut up. Come on, drink up. We can go to the caravan park bar.'

As they finished their drinks John Kelly walked over to the table. 'Do you like it living here. Quaint, isn't it.'

Denise ignored him.

'Nice flat you have,' he added.

Denise looked up and pointed to him. 'You keep away from it and me. Get it into your thick skull we are over. Finished, finito. Okay.'

He didn't answer, just turned round and walked away.

The bar in the caravan park was busy. There was a kids disco in the function room and a lot of the folk in the bar were the parents of the young boppers next door.

Lindsay-Joanne went to the bar while Denise found a table and started looking for talent.

'It's cheaper here than in the pub,' Lindsay-Joanne said

when she got back to the table.

'Couple of possibilities over there,' Denise said, her detective eye soon picking out talent.

'Out of luck there, I saw them holding hands the other day,' L-J said, bursting Denise's bubble.

As quickly as that bubble burst another floated by. Well walked over and asked if they could sit with them.

Stephen and Scott Brown were a couple of Irish brothers who were working in Dingwall and living in the caravan park. Not particularly good looking but they were full of chat, good company and willing to buy more than their share of drink.

When the bar manager rang for last orders it seemed to the girls it had only been about an hour since they walked into the bar. Truth was it was nearly three hours and they were well lubricated.

When they made it outside they paired up, Denise heading to the boy's caravan with Stephen and Lindsay-Joanne heading to her caravan with Scott. Both looking to scratch their sexual itches for the first time since the good Doctor had operated on them.

COPS AND AMBULANCES

DENISE DIDN'T even know what time it was when she left the lad's caravan, but she was smiling as she headed home. The thought of her own bed was a big lure even though she was offered a cosy sleep and the promise of more sex in the morning.

As she walked up the main road there was the approaching blue lights, no siren, as an emergency vehicle approached.

Denise stood and watched as a police car shot past. Off duty, and clearly still drunk she should have headed home, but like the Bisto kid heading for a meaty aroma she headed for her desire, to see what the trouble was.

Heading in the direction she thought the cop car went there soon followed an ambulance, blue lights on too but obviously at that time in the morning no siren either.

She guessed from the direction they went it was Churchill Avenue. Walking on up the road she wondered what had happened. A medical emergency only needed an ambulance, the fact that the police were there first made her think it was more than that.

Her guess was correct, halfway down Churchill Avenue both emergency vehicles were parked. It wasn't good, she thought.

Shit, she hadn't her warrant card with her. Still, she could explain who she was.

As she reached the house one of the bobbies approached her and stopped her getting further.

'Sorry, you can't go any further. Is this one of your workmates?'

'Sorry?'

'Are you a streetwalker like her.'

'No, I am a police officer.'

'Right. Well, you look more like a hooker to me.'

Still being slightly drunk, Denise struggled to understand what the cop was getting at. 'You are speaking to Detective Sergeant Denise Kelly,' she said, trying to sound sober at least.

'Sure. You will have a warrant card with you.'

'No. I am off duty just now.'

Just at that the ambulance crew carried out their patient.

'Oh God,' Denise said as she recognised Wendy, one of the punters from the Pheasant Plucker. She was known for her liking for men and usually a different one every week.

Her face was swollen, she had taken a right beating. Obviously with her track record with men eventually she would get hurt. Not that Denise thought it was correct.

Then it dawned on her what the young bobby was getting at, he thought she was a prostitute. 'Excuse me, what's your badge number,' she asked the young cop.

He leaned towards her and pointed to his badge. 'Two three one, P.C. David Reilly. I am based at Dingwall, not this hick town,' he answered then walked into the house.

As he walked away he turned to her. 'On your way and don't be touting for work on the way home,' he said, laughing as he went.

Denise smiled, 'You will be laughing on the other side of your face next time we meet.'

MORNING? IS IT

DENISE WAS pulled from her slumber by a loud banging on her front door. 'What the,' she said to herself, opening her eyes then closing them again.

The banging continued. Loud. Very loud. A policeman's knock. With her eyes still closed she tried to work out where she was and why the Hell was her head so sore.

Oh no, the caravan park, she started to remember. Her eyes opened enough to look at her alarm clock- just after ten o'clock.

The banging continued. She had to get up to stop it. Unsteadily she got out of bed and started for the stairs. At the top of the stairs, she realised she was naked.

The letterbox opened- 'Detective Sergeant, it's Billy, you are needed at the station.'

Her head was spinning so she sat down on the top step.

'Billy,' she called out. The shouting felt like another bang on her head. 'Billy, I will be there in half an hour.'

The letterbox opened again. 'Okay.'

Then it was quiet again. So quiet she actually dozed off again sitting there.

'Come on Denise,' she said to herself when she woke a few minutes later, 'pull yourself together. You have a duty here.'

Just before eleven o'clock Denise walked into the police station. Billy and Susan looked relieved. Susan, although only a cadet, was allowed to work with Billy at the weekend as an exception because Denise and Lindsay-Joanne both needed off the weekend off.

'What is it?' she asked.

'Wendy Lee was assaulted last night.'

Lee. Funnily enough she had never known that was Wendy's last name. 'Yes, I know.'

Billy and Susan looked at each other.

'I saw her going into the ambulance.'

'Where?'

'At her house.'

'At three o'clock?'

'Yes. So, where was she before she was attacked.'

'Saturday night she is usually in The Pheasant Plucker.'

'Right. So, we need to start our enquiries there. Right.'

Billy just nodded.

'When does The Pheasant Plucker open?' Denise asked, still not quite with it.

'Sunday, it's half past twelve.'

'Right, so why did you get me up at 10 o'clock?'

Again, Billy and Susan shared a look. This was a different Denise they knew and probably loved.

'Well, it was important,' Billy said.

'Billy, here is a thing, right. Lindsay-Joanne and I were off yesterday and today. Right.'

She waited until Billy nodded in agreement.

'So last night we went out for a drink. Right.'

She waited again until he nodded.

'We were going out to get drunk, we weren't going to the local café for an iced drink, we were going to get pissed. I have to admit we did it quite well. Now the last thing I wanted to get woken out of my slumber in what to me was the middle of the night. So, the kettle better be boiled because I am as rough as a badger's arse.'

For a third time the two other cops looked at each other then both reached for the switch on the kettle at the same time.

Denise rattled the door of The Pheasant Plucker ten minutes before opening time. Fergus opened the door with a quizzical look on his face.

'There is nobody in. Look for yourself,' he said, on the defensive.

'I would hope not, but that is not why we are here.'

'You better come in.'

Denise thought there was something strange about an empty pub. Like an empty church when the wind blows through it.

Denise walked in followed by Susan. Billy was back at the station holding the fort, or at least answering the phone if it rung.

'So, what is so important?' Fergus asked.

'Wendy Lee. Who did she leave with last night?'

'Last night she and her pal were hanging about the group of coppers that were in. They left with two of them.'

'Which two?' Denise asked.

Fergus shrugged. 'None of my business. Anyway, you lot all look the same,' he said, making an unfunny joke that only he laughed at.

'Who is her pal?' Denise asked next.

Fergus thought for a minute. 'It's Barbara something. Woods I think.'

'Where does she live?'

'Detective Sergeant, I am her publican, not her social worker.'

'Okay, Fergus, thanks for that.'

With that they left the pub. 'Hopefully Billy will know who this Barbara woman is.'

'Yes, I am always surprised when we are out how many people he knows. Seems to know everyone.'

'Yes, it's a talent, don't underestimate Billy.'

Billy was sitting drinking tea when the women walked into the station. Straight away he looked guilty, especially as Denise was in a strange mood.

'Chill Billy. Now, we are looking for your expertise.'

'What do you mean?'

'Wendy Lee's friend, Barbara somebody. Possibly Woods.'

'Babs Woods lives in Poplar Avenue, number six I think.'

'Okay, let's go.'

Denise and Susan left Billy at peace with his brew.

By the time Denise had walked the two miles to Poplar Avenue she felt a lot better. The fresh air clearing her head and actually had her feeling hungry.

'You know Susan,' she said as they walked, 'we really need

to get this guy quickly. I saw her getting carried into the ambulance, she was severely beaten.'

'Why did you see her at that time in the morning?'

'I was just heading home when I saw the police van and ambulance heading for her house. I didn't know where they were going at the time, but another good skill to have, if you could call it a skill, is to be nosey.'

Susan laughed. 'I will need to work on my nosiness skills. Wait a minute, rewind a bit, you were getting home at three o'clock from where exactly?'

'A friends caravan, we will leave it at that.'

Susan didn't speak, just gave a knowing smile.

The front garden of number six Poplar Avenue gave a good indication to the kind of tenant that lived there. It was mid-July, and the grass hadn't been cut all year, already heading to be about a foot high.

Susan knocked on the door first. They waited a minute then Denise took over. If they were going to claim they didn't hear the first knock, they couldn't say that about the second one. Half the street would have heard it.

Barbara opened the door looking like she had been pulled through a hedge backwards. Her self-dyed blond hair with black roots hadn't been combed, face not washed with the remnants of the previous night's make-up still caked on a face that had lived a life. She was naked beneath a tiny bathrobe she was pulling about her covering what little modesty she had.

'Barbara, we need to talk to you about last night.'

She rubbed at her brow. 'What about last night? I didn't do anything last night.'

'No, it's about Wendy. Somebody beat her up.'

'What? No. Where is she?'

'In hospital. Can we come in.'

'Hospital. What the fuck?'

Densie stepped forward and Barbara took the hint and walked in.

The living room was dark and Barbara put a light on before sitting down and reaching for her fags and lighter. Her hands shook as she tried to light her cigarette.

'Okay Barbara, last night. You were both in The Pheasant Plucker. I know because I saw you. What happened after that?'

'We were talking to these cops, sorry policemen, most of the night. At closing time, we copped off. Sorry, I wasn't trying to be funny. Anyway, I brought Charlie back here and Wendy and John went to hers.'

Denise suddenly had a terrible sinking feeling in the pit of her stomach. John. Her husband John. No, he wouldn't do that. Anyway, John was a common name.

'Is Wendy bad?'

'I phoned the hospital just after eleven o'clock, said she was stable.'

'I will need to go and see her,' Barbara said.

'Were the policemen staying locally?'

'Yes, they were staying in the caravan park for the weekend.'

'Okay, we will need a statement on this. Billy can come and get you when you have tidied yourself up. I will need to talk to Wendy so we can give you a lift to the hospital.'

'Okay.'

Denise then had a thought. It was a bit of a risky stroke, but she had to know for herself. She opened her handbag, took out her purse and found what she was looking for. In the notes section she had a picture. She took it out and showed it to Barbara.

'Is this John?' she asked.

Barbara took the photo and turned it to the little light in the room. 'Yes, that's him, but he is younger in the photo.'

What a stupid bastard, Denise thought.

'Right, Billy will be here in about an hour. Be ready.'

Denise got up and walked out followed by her cadet.

Denise and Susan walked back towards the police station quite quickly.

'Boss, what's happening?' Susan asked.

'I better not say,' Denise said.

'Wait a minute.'

Denise stopped and looked at Susan. 'Well.'

'You just told me to be nosey. Now I want to know what's going on and you clam up.'

Densie looked up and down the street before talking.

'Okay, I am trusting you with this, but it has to be strictly kept under your hat. If it gets out I will know it's come from you.'

Susan suddenly wondered if she did want to know what was going on. 'Okay,' she said quietly.

'The person Wendy took home last night was Detective Inspector John Kelly. My husband. The bastard who turned up at the station last week.'

'No way.'

'Now, he only took her home. Somebody else could have beat her up, but my gut tells me it was him.'

'Did he ever hit you?' Susan asked.

Denise thought it was a strange question at first, then realised it was actually a good one to ask. 'No. Never. The only time he hurt me was when he slept with a cadet in my own bed.'

'Oh God.'

'Until we talk to Wendy we won't know for certain, that's why we need to keep it quiet just now.

HOSPITAL

DENISE MADE Barbara wait in the police car with Billy while she and Susan went to see Wendy. At the reception desk of the woman's ward, she showed her warrant card and was allowed in to speak to Wendy, although she was warned not to upset her.

Wendy looked even worse than she did earlier in the morning on the gurney. She was sleeping, or just resting her swollen eyes when they went to her bedside.

Before they could speak to her a nurse appeared and pulled the curtain round the bed.

'Wendy,' Denise said quietly. She got no response.

'Wendy Lee, it's Denise Kelly, the policewoman,' she spoke into her ear.

Her eyes flickered and opened slightly.

'Wendy, we need to get the person who did this to you. Do you know who it was?'

She nodded slightly.

'Who was it?' was all Denise could ask her; she couldn't say anything to lead her.

'A guy from the pub I took him home.'

Denise got the same sinking feeling in her stomach. It was so unlike her husband, but it sounded very much like it was him that did it.

'Did he not say his second name?'

'No. Just said he was a cop.'

'Why did he attack you?'

'He asked for anal. I don't do that. He started putting it in there. It was sore and I pulled away. He said if I didn't do anal he would hurt me. I told him to get out and he slapped me. I slapped him back then he just battered me.'

She spoke slowly and deliberately. Denise was sure it was sore for her just talking and admired her for it.

It all seemed a bit strange to her, John had never asked her for anal sex before. In fact, he was dead against it, said it was what poofters did, and he wasn't a poofter.

While Wendy stopped for a rest Denise took the photo of her husband out.

'Is this him?'

Wendy opened her eyes a bit more then had to concentrate to get the image clear in her head. She started nodding her head then tears formed in her eyes then ran down her face.

'Sorry Wendy, but I need you to say it.'

'It was that bastard,' she managed to say.

'Right, we will leave you alone now. I will write up a statement and bring it in tomorrow.'

Densie put the picture back in her purse and they walked round the bed and slipped out the end of the curtain.

After telling the nurse they were off she checked that Barbara could go in and see her. The nurse said it was ok for a short while.

Walking back to the car Susan asked Denise a question.

'Is it okay if I ask you a personal question, Denise?'

'You can ask, but I might not answer it.'

'Okay. Why do you carry a picture of your ex in your purse?

Do you still fancy him?'

'What? No, definitely not, it's the opposite really. The reason I carry the picture is to remind me not to get involved with an arsehole like him ever again.'

'Thanks for telling me.'

When they reached the car Barbara was already getting out.

'How is she?' she asked.

'She doesn't look good, but they are confident she will make a full recovery, nothing broken. Before you go in, the nurse said you won't be able to stay long. Remember we aren't a taxi service.

However, if you are only ten minutes we will wait and take you back to Glenfurny,' Denise said.

'No, I won't be waiting. I just want her to know I am there for her and will be when she gets out.'

With that Barbara left, tottering on high heels across the car park to the hospital entrance.

Ten minutes later Barbara reemerged. She was crying. By the time she reached the car and got in she was still weeping.

'Upsetting isn't it,' Susan said to her as she sat in the back seat beside her.

'No, it isn't that. When we headed back from the pub the guys told us to pick which one of them we took home. Wendy picked John. If she had picked Charlie I would be in there now.'

'Don't worry Barbara, we will get the bastard that did it.

Denise knocked on the door of Lindsay-Joanne's caravan door. L-J opened it wearing a housecoat and her other bedclothes on. She looked surprised to see Denise there, especially with a bag which looked like it had clothes in it.

'Hi. I am looking for a big favour.'

'Come in.'

Densie walked in but didn't put the bag down. 'I am looking for somewhere to sleep tonight.'

'Why?'

She explained the events of the previous day and recalled that her husband knew where she stayed.

'Until he is behind bars I won't feel safe sleeping in the flat.'

'Sure, there is a spare room. I will just need to take my clothes off the bed.'

'Thanks. At least you will get a lift to work tomorrow,' Denise said with a laugh.

BACK TO WORK ON MONDAY,
FEELS LIKE NEVER BEEN AWAY.

DENISE UNLOCKED the police station front door and walked in. First thing she needed to do was phone the Chief Constable. That, she knew, would be embarrassing.

They were in the office probably too early to call him, but Denise wanted it over with. In fact, she wanted the whole episode over and done with. She hadn't slept much the night before and not only because of the strange bed, it bothered her so much that her husband had committed GBH on another woman.

Densie went through to the back office. There was still a background whiff of deep heat, she would have to suffer it.

The number rang. As it rung on she was ready to hang up when it was answered. She had been right, too early for his secretary, it the Chief Inspector himself.

'Morning sir, sorry to bother you, but I need to talk to you personally. It's D.S. Denise Kelly from Glenfurny.'

'Is this about maternity leave,' he asked seriously, no hint of humour.

There was a pregnant pause until she realised he was joking. At least she thought he was joking. 'No sir, it's a serious matter. In fact, it is a very serious matter.'

'Is it urgent, because I am mobile all day today.'

'Will you be near Dingwall? I could meet you there.'

'Hold on till I check.' There was a silence, and Denise could hear him turning pages, no doubt checking through his diary. 'Fortunately, I am scheduled to be there at one o'clock. How long will the talk take?'

'Five minutes tops, sir.'

'Okay, meet me at Dingwall police station at ten to one.' With that the phone went dead.

She went through to the front office. Her tea was out in the cup.

'Thanks Lindsay-Joanne. I will be heading out at twelve o'clock in the yellow peril. I will leave you the squad car in case you need it.'

'Are you seeing the boss?'

'Yes, I need to explain how you became pregnant with you practically a virgin.'

'Yes,' she laughed, 'as much a virgin as you.'

Denise sat in reception at Dingwall police station just after half past twelve. She had a folder with the statements from Wendy and Barbara. For all they had spoken that morning Denise still felt anxious about seeing the boss. Still, she was early, that was a plus point.

Five minutes earlier than agreed Chief Inspector John McKelvie strode into the reception area where Denise was sitting.

She gave a half smile, the thing she admired about him was his presence. He walked into a room, and it became instantly obvious that he was a man of power.

'Ah, D.S. Kelly. Lost a bit of weight I see,' was his opening gambit.

'I eh,' was all she could say as a flush came to her cheeks.

'Right, we better have this private conversation.' He turned to the civilian on duty at the reception desk. 'Hello dear. We need a private place to have a conversation for a few minutes, what do you have?'

'Hold on,' she said and disappeared to the back office.

Within seconds the door opened, and a flustered looking desk sergeant appeared.

'Good morning sir, ma'am, come this way,' he said and led them down a corridor.

He opened the door to a small interview room and put the light on. 'If you need anything else just give me a shout.'

The room was basic, just a table and two chairs either side of it. They sat opposite each other.

Denise put the file on the table and pushed it towards him.

'On Saturday night, or rather the early hours of Sunday morning a woman was assaulted, pretty badly, by a man she said was a police officer. From my inquiries the person responsible was Detective Inspector John Kelly, my husband. As this is the case I cannot continue with this case.'

The Chief lifted the cover and looked at the first page but said nothing. Even after he scanned the information he still never spoke.

'Wait a minute, do you think I set this all up? I don't love John anymore, but I don't hate him. The guy that battered this woman wasn't the John I loved and married.'

'No, it's not that. I know your work and I also know this report will have everything I need to pass on. No, I was wondering whether the case stays here in Dingwall or goes to Inverness.'

'There is one thing that isn't included there, when I went to the hospital this morning and got the victim to sign her statement she mentioned white powder, thinks he might have been taking drugs.'

'That would make sense, we are seeing a growing trend of people becoming violent after snorting drugs. I would think this should stay in Dingwall. The detectives here are good guys. Yes, that is what I will do.'

The Chief Inspector closed the file. 'Do you want to talk about Saturday and what I would call conduct unbecoming of a police officer.'

'Look sir, it was just a joke, but there was a reason for it. Doctor Grant Jamieson asked my friend and myself out on dates, separately of course, under the pretext he was single and available. When we found out he was engaged we thought it would be funny to gatecrash his wedding and show him off for the rat he was.'

'Okay, that's fair enough, I suppose I don't blame you. Now I will progress this immediately,' he said, tapping the file.

'Could you ask them to inform me when he is arrested. He told me he knows where I live, and I am scared he turns up there. I am sleeping at a friend's place until I feel safe enough to return to my flat.'

'Sure, that will be done. Anything else?'

'No, sir.'

The Chief got up and walked out while Denise followed. When they got to the reception area John McKelvie turned and shook her hand. 'Keep up the good work Denise.'

'Thank you sir,' Denise said then started to walk out when she remembered something. She waited until the Chief went through to the detective's offices then approached the reception desk again.

'Is P.C. David Reilly on duty today?'

The civilian receptionist thought. 'I think he is, hold on.'

She disappeared into the back office. A few minutes David appeared.

'Can I help you?' he asked.

'Can we go through here for a minute.'

'Sure,' he said and followed her into the room she had just left.

Denise produced her warrant card. 'You don't seem to recognise me. As I told you on Sunday morning I am a Detective Sergeant.'

A worried look appeared on his face; he swallowed hard as it dawned on him who she was.

'If I made this official you would get a reprimand I am sure. However, if I get an apology and a promise you won't jump to conclusions in future that will be the end of it.'

'No please don't report it, I am so sorry. To be honest I was so tired. My wife is pregnant and hasn't been sleeping. When I am home from work I end up staying up with her. I was really tired on Saturday night. I promise I won't jump to conclusions again. In fact, to be honest, even in the state you were in you looked quite hot.'

'Right, I think we should leave it at that David. Good luck with the birth of your child.'

With that she walked out of the room and out of the station.

RELIEF

ALL OF the next day Denise was stressed. If John realised the cops were onto him he might run to her, either for refuge or retribution. Not that she had done anything wrong but who knows how a deranged mind works. Especially if he was doing drugs.

The call came just after four o'clock. The D.I. leading the case told Denise his name but in her haste to find out the result of the investigation wasn't concentrating in the other details. The main thing was John had been arrested and charged with sexual assault. His career was over.

'Bad news, Lindsay-Joanne, you have lost a roommate,' she told her as soon as she was off the phone.

'Oh, that's a shame, we were getting on so well.'

'Yeah, that would be okay until you wanted to bring a guy home, and I would have to lie in the room next to you listening to the banging.'

'Banging?'

'Yes, the headboard against the wall.'

'I suppose so. Scott said he might come round one night this week.'

'Lucky you,' Denise said with a smile.

Denise had a load of washing and ironing to catch up on after staying at Lindsay-Joanne's caravan for two nights. Halfway through her chores she heard a knock on the door.

Even though she had heard her husband was safely behind bars in Inverness she wasn't taking any chances and grabbed her truncheon.

Opening the door slowly she was relieved to see it was her landlady who answered.

'Hi, Denise, is everything ok. You haven't been here for a few days.'

'Oh, Marion, I am sorry, I should have told you. A friend wasn't well, and I stayed over for a few nights to look after her.'

'Oh, right. Thought it might have been something to do with the assault in town on Saturday night.'

'No, nothing to do with that. I was working on that case though. The good news is the guy that did it is behind bars.'

'Oh, that' i good news.'

Denise wondered if she should tell her more but decided against it.

'What was wrong with your friend?' Marion asked, throwing Denise for a few seconds.

'She is pregnant and was struggling with the effects. Her husband works away on the oil rigs, and she needed company.'

'Would I know her?'

'No, she lives in Dingwall, just moved up from Glasgow.'

'Oh, right, then. As long as everything is ok.'

'Yes, thanks.'

Denise closed the front door and felt so guilty for not being honest with Marion. There again if she told her the truth she might want her out of the flat.

ROBBERY

EARLY AUGUST and the sun appeared and decided it didn't want to leave, except for a few hours each night.

Monday morning and Denise was on duty with Billy. With the heat being on the only calls they were getting were about rowdy neighbours and mischievous kids.

'Think we should go to Samson's shop for an ice lolly?' Denise asked.

'No, they say the best thing to keep you cool is a cup of tea.'

Denise shook her head, but the conversation was cut short by the phone ringing.

'What, okay, we will be right there,' Denise said. 'Samson's quick, there's been a robbery.'

'Where are the car keys?' Billy said.

Denise had pulled her jacket on and was already round the counter. 'For God's sake Billy, it's a hundred yards down the road, run.'

'What if we need to chase them?'

Denise just shook her head and ran out.

In the shop the assistant was alone and sitting crying.

'Hi Laura. What happened?'

Laura was visibly shaking. 'This guy walked in.'

They were disturbed by the bell clanging announcing a customer had arrived.

'Shops closed at the minute!' Denise called out.

'I'm in a hurry,' the elderly gent snapped back at her.

'This is a crime scene, if you don't want to be a suspect leave now!' she called, letting him know who was in charge.

Just at that Billy drew up in the panda car outside the shop.

'Hold on a moment Laura,' Denise said. She stepped out of the shop just as Billy was getting out of the car.

'Right, don't let anyone else come in the shop,' she ordered.

Laura had stopped crying when Denise returned.

'Okay, Laura, where were you?'

'The shop was empty, and this guy came in. Big guy, over six foot and muscly. I didn't notice at first that he had a like polo neck covering his face and a woollen hat on. Next thing I saw a big knife. He said empty the till and you won't get hurt.'

'You emptied the till then.'

Laura nodded. 'Hugh told us to do that, don't risk getting hurt he said.'

'Yes, safest thing to do. How long were you in the shop on your own?'

'Half an hour,' she answered. 'Hugh always goes out of the shop at ten o'clock if he has deliveries.'

'Would you know the guy again if you saw him?'

Laura shook her head. 'It all happened so fast, and I was so scared.'

'It's okay. Don't blame yourself. How much did he get, do you reckon?'

'About three hundred pounds.'

'Wow, that sounds a lot.'

'Hugh usually takes it to the bank on a Monday, but it's closed today, Bank Holiday.'

The shop door opened. Denise was ready to give Billy a bollocking until she saw it was Hugh Samson, the store's owner.

'What's happened?'

'Laura was held up at knifepoint,' Denise said.

'Oh, God no. Are you okay?' he asked her.

She started crying again.

'Just the shock,' Denise said.

Hugh walked over towards the till. 'Are you going to get it brushed for fingerprints?' he asked Denise.

'Why? It was Laura who opened it?'

'Right enough.' He opened the till then took the drawer out. Reaching in he grabbed a large handful of notes. 'At least he didn't get these,' he said smiling.

'How much would have been in the till then; you know the notes?'

About a hundred quid,' Hugh answered.

Out of the corner of her eye Denise saw a disappointed look on Laura's face.

'Right, Billy and I will do a quick reccy around town see if we see anyone hanging about that resembles the description of the robber.'

Billy drove. The streets were quite quiet, either people were too hot and hiding indoors or out their backs in paddling pools or sunbathing. Nobody matching the description of the perpetrator.

'Right, back to the shop. I reckon the guy must have cased the joint.'

'What do you mean cased the joint?' Billy asked.

'What I mean is he must have been watching the shop, noting the comings and goings, knowing when Laura was alone in the shop.'

'Yes, that sound about right.'

Denise smiled at his vote of confidence. 'Then I will need to phone Dingwall, see if they have had any similar cases.'

'Yes, I would do that too.'

Denise sat in the back office writing up the report of that day's events. Doing door-to-door hadn't revealed a single thing. Surely somebody would have seen a big guy hanging around, especially if it was a stranger.

Just as she finished writing it up the door was banged then Billy rushed in.

'There's been another hold-up down town. Cheryl Johnstone's hardware shop. Somebody's been stabbed.'

'Well don't just stand there, get the car.'

Billy drove the car like Jackie Stewart, Densie had to hold onto the side of the chair as he shot down the road. Braking to a halt outside Johnstone's hardware shop Denise was never as glad to get out of a car in her life.

The ambulance hadn't arrived and Ian Johnstone, Cheryl's son, was lying on the shop floor. The bleeding from his stomach staunched by a neighbour holding a towel against it.

'Do you know first aid?' Denise asked the woman.

'Yes, I was a nurse.'

The sound of a siren filled the air, help had arrived. Within five minutes Ian was on a stretcher and on his way to Dingwall hospital. Ian's girlfriend, Kim Goudie, who worked in the shop with him, went with him. Cheryl said she would join them later.

'So, what happened?'

'This guy came in and he had a pullover on which he pulled over his face. He also had a woollen hat on. Next thing he pulled out a knife and told Ian to empty the till. Stupid sod wanted to be a have a go hero and went for him. Next thing we know he stabbed him. That was what he told us; we were in the back shop doing stocktaking at the time. Always do on a Monday afternoon so we can sort out our orders for the wholesalers.'

'Did he describe him?'

'He said he was smaller and skinnier than him, that was why he tried to get the knife off him.'

'Who would know you did the stocktaking on a Monday afternoon?'

'Just us and anybody who worked here before.'

'Is there many on that list?'

'Now, let me think. Kim, that's Kim Gouide Ian's girlfriend. Before her it was Laura Cox, she left here two months ago. Before her it was Steph Muir.'

'Laura Cox, is that the girl who works in Samson's shop.'

'Yes.'

'Why did she leave?'

'Leave, no, she was left.'

'What do you mean?'

'I sacked her. She was stocktaking for herself. Stock was going missing and neither Ian nor I would take it. Couldn't prove it that was why I didn't report it to you.'

'Did you tell Hugh Samson?'

Cheryl shook her head. 'Never liked him, thought they deserved each other.'

Denise shook her head. 'Right, I will check with Dingwall, see if there has been a spate of robberies there.'

As she was leaving the phone rang. Cheryl answered it.

'No. No way.'

'What?'

'They say I need to get to the hospital right away.'

Denise and Billy got back in the car. 'Back to the station Billy. No motor racing.'

'Okay,' Billy said disappointedly.

OH NO!

DENISE STAYED late writing up the report of the robbery at Johnstone's hardware shop. She was working the next day but in the police you never knew what the next day would hold and liked to start with a clean slate.

Dinner would be out of the chippy she decided as she went to put the lights out after six o'clock. The phone rang. She walked round and answered it.

Cheryl Johnstone was on the other end. 'He's dead,' she squealed.

'Oh no!' Denise replied.

'Ian's been murdered, you need to catch the killer.'

'Yes, we will.'

The phone went dead.

Denise went back through to the back office and phoned Dingwall; they would be getting involved now.

Next morning Denise called at the police station first thing and filled Lindsay-Joanne in with the details of what had happened the day before. She also told her she suspected Laura Cox had lied, and she could have been involved in both robberies.

'How do you think we get to the bottom of it?' Denise asked, testing her.

'Speak to Samson first. Find out if any money's gone missing since she started working there.'

'Yes, that would be my first move. I am going to phone him and ask him to nip up here.'

Hugh Samson arrived twenty minutes later.

'Have you got him?' he asked, smiling.

'No, I am afraid not. Unfortunately, it looks like Laura got off lightly. Did you not hear Ian Johnstone got stabbed. He died last night.'

'Oh my God,' he said. 'She could have been killed.'

'Yes, maybe. How has Laura been doing?'

'Doing? Fine, how?'

'Just something Cheryl Johnstone said to me yesterday. Things going missing.'

'No, I trust her implicitly. Anyway, Cheryl said she was trustworthy.'

'Did she now. Has Laura got a boyfriend; do you know?'

'Yes. Never seen him though.'

'Do you have a name for him?'

Hugh rubbed at his brow. 'Daniel something. Let me think, Daniel Burns. I am sure that's it.'

'Local boy?'

'Yes, I think so.'

'Cheers Hugh, we will let you know if there are any updates.'

When Hugh left Denise went over and got the keys for the panda car. 'Come on, we are off.'

'I thought this was your day off,' Lindsay-Joannes said.

'Not when there is a crime to solve.'

'It's Dingwall's case now.'

'Well, would it not be good to solve it before they get here?'

'I suppose so. Where are we going then?' Lindsay-Joanne

said, as she struggled to get her jacket on quickly.

'Billy's. The A to Z of folk in the town.'

Just as they headed out the station door Susan Maxwell appeared.

'What's going on?' she asked.

'Nothing for you to worry about, you just man the phone,' Denise said.

Susan shrugged and walked past them. She was just glad she hadn't been pulled for being late.

Billy was still in bed when they knocked on his front door. He appeared, after his mother called him down, wearing a pair of stripey pyjamas.

'Sorry to bother you, Billy, we are looking for Daniel Burns. Do you know him?'

'Is that Ann and Bert's son. Toerag he is. They live in Oldmaid Street.'

'Okay, you can go back to bed,' Denise said.

'Sorry, I was up all night with my mum. She wasn't well.'

'Oh, right,' Denise said, thinking she seemed fine when she was yelling up to him.

Oldmaid Street was an avenue of private houses in the oldest part of town. They found the house after asking a few neighbours and walked up to the front of the house.

'You knock, I will catch him if he runs out the back door,' Denise said.

'You what,' Lindsay-Joanne said.

'Trust me,' her boss said.

Denise walked down the side of the house and gave L-J the

thumbs up when she reached the back of the house.

Lindsay-Joanne knocked on the door. A minute later Ann opened the door. L-J showed flashed her warrant card.

'Mrs. Burns, can I have a word with your son Daniel.'

Ann turned and shouted up the stairs. 'Daniel, the police are here, want a word.'

'Suddenly there was a thundering down the stairs then the lad headed back through the house instead of coming to the front door.

Within seconds there was a yell from the back door. Lindsay-Joanne ran round and found Denise with Daniel in a headlock.

'We only wanted a word,' Denise said, holding them as her assistant snapped the handcuffs on his wrists.

Denise and Lindsay-Joanne stood next to Daniel in the cell in the police station.

'Okay, Daniel, you are going to spend a long time in one of these if you don't start talking,' Lindsay-Joanne said. She was being the good cop.

Daniel didn't speak.

'Was it Laura? She knew the inside information, about when Hugh was out of the shop.'

Daniel still didn't speak.

'Look, you aren't some criminal mastermind, you are just a little runt going about holding up defenceless shopkeepers with a big knife. What a fucking coward,' Denise, bad cop, said, jumping in.

'It wasn't my idea. Laura handed me the money when I went in the shop. Then she said it would have been Kim Goudie in the shop, but it wasn't, it was Ian, and the stupid git tried to get the knife off me. He pulled it and stabbed himself.'

'Why did you not tell us this?'

'Laura told me to burn all my clothes, that's what I did. She said they had no proof, but it's in my head. I didn't sleep last night.' Then he erupted into tears.

While he wasn't looking the two women high fived each other.

NOT HAPPY

DENISE AND Lindsay-Joanne were widely congratulated for getting a result in the Ian Johnstone case. Everybody was, it seemed, happy that there was a quick conclusion to the case. That was until the front door of the station burst open a fortnight after Ian died.

'What the fuck is going on?' Cheryl Johnstone said, pointing a finger at Denise.

Billy, her partner that day, got up from his chair, ready to defend her.

'What's wrong Cheryl?' she asked.

'What's wrong? What the fuck is wrong? Manslaughter. Ian was fucking murdered. Murdered. Yet you allow that little shit Burns get off with a lesser charge of manslaughter.'

'Cheryl, that side of it is out of my hands. Once we arrest him it is up to the procurator fiscal to decide if he is charged and if so what with.'

'Bullshit. You and I both know Ian was murdered by Daniel Burns.'

'As I said, it doesn't matter what we think or know, as I said it's up to the procurator fiscal. The other thing you need to take into consideration is if Daniel is charged with murder there is always a chance with a good defendant he could get off with it altogether. With him admitting to manslaughter you definitely get a result, and he is behind bars.'

Some of it seemed to have sunk in and Cheryl calmed a bit.

'If you don't agree with it, take it up with the prosecutor fiscal, I am sure they will tell you the same thing I have just said,' Denise continued.

'Well, well I am not happy,' she said and stormed out, trying to slam the front door, thwarted by the door closer.

'Well done boss,' Billy said.

'Just got to work with the head, Billy.'

MURDER, MYSTERY

'HOW DO you fancy going on a murder mystery night?' Lindsay-Joanne asked Denise one day in the office.

'A what, a murder mystery night?'

'Yeah, it's the latest craze. The stately homes are doing it to try to get money to repair roofs and stuff like that. Basically, somebody is supposed to get murdered, and the others have to guess who did it.'

'Sounds like a busman's holiday, well busman's night out to me,' Denise said.

'That's the thing, we must be certainties to win it with our knowledge.'

'I don't think it's my kind of thing.'

'Remember our last night out, that turned out ok.'

'Apart from the serious assault by my husband.'

'Yeah, but he is in the jail now. He won't be the guilty one there. Look, it's only a tenner a head, including a three-course meal and I will even pay it. Think I owe you that much anyway.'

'How can I say no. When is it?'

'Next Saturday. Your weekend off, I will swap with Susan.'

Susan, the cadet, had passed her probationary and was able to work both weekends and nightshifts if required.

'Okay, I will go even if it's just to keep you company and give you a chance of winning,' Denise laughed.

As usual, before a night out, Lindsay-Joanne headed to Denise's flat for a drink before heading to the murder mystery night. After downing half a bottle of wine each, they were in a taxi headed for Glenfurny house.

'Wow, this place looks amazing,' Lindsay-Joanne said as they got out the taxi. She had never been up to the big house. Denise had, but only during the day. At night, all lit up as it was, it looked very imposing.

Other cars and taxis were arriving and there was a buzzing atmosphere in the air.

Their tickets were checked then they were shown straight into the dining room. The dining table was huge and seated for over 20 people.

After being seated they were immediately offered a drink.

'Wow, this is swanky,' Lindsay-Joanne said.

'Sure is. If we get a three-course meal we won't be able to detect anything.'

Just at that moment Denise looked up and saw somebody walking in the room she recognised and dreaded seeing, Cheryl Johnstone was walking in with another woman. It was only a month since her son was killed, Denise was surprised she was socialising so soon, she would still have been in mourning for her son, if she ever has one.

'Oh no,' she said quietly.

'What?' L-J whispered back.

'Look who just walked in.'

Lindsay-Joanne looked over and saw her. 'Oh God, no. Hopefully she will be seated at the other end of the table.' They tried not to be seen watching, but the worst possible thing happened, they were seated straight opposite them.

Denise and Lindsay-Joanne turned their chairs to face each other, rather than face forward.

Luckily for them the table filled up quickly after that. Not that quickly that they had any of their white wine left.

There was a tinkling of a glass at one end of the table and all eyes turned to see what it was.

Cameron Stuart, the owner of the house looked every bit the wealthy landowner dressed as he was in full highland dress with the red Royal Stuart tartan. Large as he was, his voice matched his appearance, and he didn't need a public address system when he spoke.

'Good evening good folks and welcome to my humble abode Glenfurny house and our very first murder mystery night. I am Cameron Stuart, and I will be your host, at least for a short time. I will now hand you over to your host for tonight, John Gough of the Glenfurny players.'

John Gough headed to the top of the table, as he did so he instructed two of the other players to hand out pieces of paper that would turn out to be their entry forms for the contest to guess who the killer was.

'Thank you Cameron, you seem very jovial for someone who will soon be dead.'

The host laughed and some of the guests laughed along.

'You see, unfortunately Cameron will be the victim of the crime this evening. I will introduce you to the five suspects tonight.'

John pointed to each of the suspects who identified themselves by their character.

'I am Emily Coates, and I am the housekeeper here.'

'I am June Brown, and I am the cook.

'I am Nick Peston, and I am the gamekeeper.

'I am Larry Wicks, and I am the gardener.

'I am Stuart Urquart, and I am the estate manager.'

'Thank you folks, I am sure you will agree with me they look too nice to be killers, but one of them is. Now two of the players are handing out slips of paper that you complete after you have toured the house and decided who will be the killer and with what weapon. Through the house there are possible weapons or clues in every room, except those clearly marked as out of bounds. After dinner you will have thirty minutes to tour the house, check the clues then make your decision. Winner will win a prize and free entry to the next event here.

The meal will now be served.'

The hush that prevailed was suddenly broken by a ripple of applause then each group that were there all started talking at once.

Denise looked at the slip of paper. There were twelve choices of weapon marked down and five suspects.

'Looks like a crock of shit,' she said.

'Well, at least the wine is good quality, we can always get pissed,' Lindsay-Joanne said.

The starters arrived and it was pate with toast. There was partial silence again as everybody, well almost everybody, concentrated on eating. The only noise was the cutlery scratching on plates.

Cheryl Johnstone waited on the silence to make her remark.

'I don't see a box for stabbed in the back by your local female detective,' she said, loudly, to her friend. Loudly enough for everybody in earshot to hear clearly.

Her friend just laughed while they both stared over, looking for a reaction.

The two cops continued concentrating on their food and didn't look over. 'I would like to smack her,' Lindsay-Joanne said beneath her breath to Denise.

'Join the club,' Denise said back.

They finished their meals without any further distractions, Cheryl keeping quiet. Just before they got up to tour the house she sniped again.

'Well Denise, this will show you up when you can't solve a simple murder like this.'

'Who says I won't solve it?' she nipped back.

Denise and Lindsay-Joanne hung back, waiting to see which way Cheryl and her friend went so that they could go the opposite way. Sure, they would expect cross paths at some point, they would deal with that.

First room was the library. On one of the tables was a large, sharp letter opener with a label marked clue.

Denise picked it up and laughed. 'Why don't we get labels with clue on them when we investigate a crime,' before handing it to Lindsay-Joanne.

'Denise, why don't we just go. We have had our meal, and a few drinks. The thing is, if we don't get it right Cheryl Johnstone would have a field day. If we do get it right they will be saying we shouldn't have been allowed to enter.'

'You are right, but if we walk away they will use that against us in the future. What we do is go with the flow then tell the organiser because we are police officers we don't want to enter the competition.'

'That,' Lindsay-Joanne said, with a slight alcoholic pause, 'is why you are the boss.'

They walked through the rest of the huge house, scanning the clues.

'It's right what we said earlier,' Lindsay-Joanne said, 'this is a load of shit. You could pick any two and have as much chance of getting it right as somebody who wasn't even here.'

'Yes, they will need to rethink it if they do it again.'

They managed to get round the house without bumping

into Cheryl Johnston and her friend. However, they were hardly back at the table when they arrived back.

The table had been cleared and a bar set up in the corner of the room. Denise took the chance to get away from the table and offered to get the drinks.

As she made it back with two white wines John Gouch announced the forms needed filled in.

Denise took her form and quickly marked off two boxes at random. She smiled as she handed over her form.

'Who did you tick off?' Lindsay-Joanne asked.

'Don't know,' Denise said with a smile. 'What about you?'

'The gardener, by hitting him with the golf club.'

'As good a guess as any,' Denise said with a smile.

Dong. The dinner gong rang out.

'That's it,' John the organiser said. 'The murder has been committed.'

As soon as he said it the piercing noise of a gunshot rang out from what sounded like an upstairs bedroom. It was joined a few seconds later by the sound of a second shot.

'I don't remember seeing a gun' Denise said. Looking quickly at John she saw from his face the shooting was nothing to do with the murder mystery night. She quickly looked round the room, not looking to see who was there, looking to see who wasn't.

The table seemed full, the organiser and four of the suspects were all there. The only person she couldn't account for was Stuart Urquhart, the estate manager. Denise had met him previously which was why she remembered him.

'Let's go,' Denise said to Lindsay-Joanne, who realised like her it wasn't part of the show.

They knew the noise came from upstairs, so they headed for

the main staircase and hurried up it. They stopped at the top of the stairs to grab a breath and try to work out where the shots came from.

They walked quickly along the corridor scanning each room until they found the source of the shots. Lying in one of the bedrooms, in a pool of blood, lay the lifeless body of Cameron Stuart.

Two bullet holes clearly visible, one to the chest, one to the head. Denise put a hand to his neck. But it was obvious he was already dead.

'Oh God,' Lindsay-Joanne said, breaking the deadly silence. The only noise the rattling of rain against the bedroom window.

Denise got up and started heading back to the dining room. 'Come on, let's get back to the dining room. We need back-up immediately. First thing we need is to get a record of who was here. We aren't going to be able to interview everybody tonight, so we need them out of the way. Except the staff of course.'

There was a lot of chatter in the dining room when the two detectives walked in. Denise stood at the top of the table and raised her arms. 'Silence please. Would somebody call the police.'

Looking up she saw Stuart Urquart had appeared at the back of the room. He put his hand up. 'What is it?' he asked.

'Cameron Stuart has been murdered.'

There were gasps of surprised. Denise kept her gaze on Urquart. He looked surprised, but not shocked.

He hurried past her to get to a phone.

Denise asked John Gouch if he had a notepad they could use, which he said he had.

'Okay, as you were all in the room here when the shots went off you are not suspects, but in some small ways you may be witnesses. You can all leave after giving all contact details to myself or Lindsay-Joanne. That's the guests, I mean. The staff and players will need to stay a bit longer.'

Lindsay-Joanne was given the notepad and a pen and quickly a queue formed. Who wouldn't want to get out of a house where a killer could still be lurking. To ensure nobody tried to sneak out Denise went out and took up a station at the front door.

Looking out she could see the night had turned dirty, heavy showers had been battering the front of the house, already forming puddles on the gravel.

After five minutes Stuart Urquart walked up to Denise.

'I can take over here if you like,' he said.

'No, I need to be here when the reinforcements arrive,' she said, thinking quickly. After all, she suspected him, what if he had an accomplice he could let sneak out undetected.

'Okay. Anything else I can do?'

'Sure. Get any of the other staff, you know kitchen staff and waitresses, to wait in the dining room with the others.'

Stuart nodded.

'By the way, where were you when the shots were fired?'

'Oh, I was out the front of the building. Somebody going round the rooms for the game reported seeing somebody in the bushes. A man in dark clothes.'

'That's fine. If you could get the staff sorted.'

Urquart nodded and walked away.

Denise shook her head. If he had been out checking through bushes for a dark stranger he would have been wet, his clothes were bone dry. She smelt a rat, a big one.

'Wait a minute, who won?' a drunk guy shouted out, bringing a bit of levity to a serious situation.

John Gouch panicked and held his hands up. Before he could give an answer Denise stepped in.

'Do you not think there are more serious things to worry about here!' she shouted, shutting him and anybody else who wanted to be funny.

THE CAVALRY ARRIVE

BY THE time the first taxi arrived Lindsay-Joanne had the names, addresses and contact details of almost all of the guests. The taxis were soon followed by two panda cars with blues and twos. Hardly needed in the grounds of the big house Denise thought.

There was also a big Rover car with the detectives in it. D.I. Morton stepped out of the car and walked over to Denise.

'On nights are we?' he asked.

'No, off duty. I was at a murder mystery night that has ended in a real murder.'

Morton shook his head slightly. 'Trouble seems to follow you around. So, who is the unlucky contestant?'

'No, it's the host, the owner of Glenfurny House, Cameron Stuart. Shot twice.'

People were starting to walk out and wait for their lifts or taxis, so the Detectives walked down the hallway away from possible listening ears. They were joined by Nelson's partner, it wasn't D.C. Neal, another young 'tec.

Denise gave him a quick once over, not the kind of guy you kicked out of bed for farting she thought. Then she remembered the photo in her purse- no job she recalled.

'I haven't had a chance to look about upstairs, I've been making sure nobody got out without leaving their details. Detective Constable Connor is gathering their info in the dining room.'

'Right, let's go see the body.'

They walked up the big staircase to the upstairs. It was deadly quiet, the only noise as they walked down the corridor was Nelson's breathing.

The body was exactly where Denise had seen it earlier.

Nelson walked over and examined the bullet wounds. He shook his head as he turned to face the other two who waited at the room door. 'Looks like a professional hit,' he said.

'Or an ex-army man,' Denise said, strengthening her thought Urquart was responsible.

'Forensics were contacted but they are coming from Inverness, could be more than an hour before they get here,' Nelson said. 'Barry, you stay here and guard the body until I can get a plod to take over from you.'

The other two walked back downstairs. Halfway down on the landing Nelson stopped. 'You suspect somebody,' he said.

'How do you know?'

'I picked up vibes from you the last time we worked together, so, what do you think?'

Denise looked around to make sure nobody could hear. 'I am sure Urquart is our man. He is ex-army, he was one of the few folk not in the dining room when the shots were fired and he said he was outside at the time, yet it was raining and he was bone dry.'

'Right, we go softly softly, interview the other staff and find out if there was an issue between the two men.'

'Okay boss.'

'Are you okay? You look tired.'

'Yeah, well I had a lot of drink tonight, I've been running on adrenalin, might be running out now.'

'Give me until the forensics arrive then I will get you home,'

Nelson said.

'Sure.'

The dining room was almost empty of punters, the Glenfurny players and staff were all there. Lindsay-Joanne looked the way Denise was starting to feel.

Denise put a hand round her shoulder. 'Not the night out we expected, eh. Still, we did get a murder. Detective Inspector Nelson says he will get us a lift home when the forensics team get here.'

Nelson had sent one of the uniforms up to guard the body and Detective Constable Barry Neal joined them, giving them two teams of two to start initial interviews.

Denise and Barry took one of the staff, the cook while Nelson and Lindsay-Joanne interviewed the head of house.

Denise and Barry took Mandy Rice into the library. Denise checked the doors were firmly closed before starting the interview. They sat on straight back wooden chairs with Mandy sitting opposite the other two.

'Mandy, as you know your boss, Cameron, has been shot. Did he have any enemies?' Denise asked, getting straight to the point.

'Not that I know about,' she said.

'Is there a Mrs. Stuart?'

'No. Well, not any more. She left about eight years ago. They are divorced now.'

'Amicable?'

'No, she took him to the cleaners, that's why he was doing this night, to get money in to help with the upkeep of the estate.'

'Has he been making cutbacks?' Denise asked.

'Yes, we have all had to pull her belts in.'

'Anything that caused friction?'

'Well, there was the pheasants.'

Denise kept silent, hoping Mandy would add to what she said.

'He decided this year not to keep the pheasant rearing and stop the pheasant shoot in August.'

'I take it he fell out with the gamekeeper.'

'No, the estate manager, Stuart Urquart.'

'Yes, but that would have been earlier in the year.'

'No, Urquart kept bringing it up, telling him he could still buy birds, he had a mate who could supply them. Cameron just kept saying no.'

'Okay, well I think that's enough for tonight, well this morning. Bet you will be glad to get home.'

'Yes. My husband will be thinking I am having an affair.'

'Right, we have all your details, if we need to speak again we will obviously be in touch.'

Mandy got up and walked out. Alone, Denise felt a hand on hers.

'You look really tired,' Barry said.

Denise felt a little spark of electricity between them. Maybe it was a combination of tiredness and the drink wearing off but if he offered to take her to bed there and then she would have.

'Forensics are here,' Nelson shouted in.

Denise pulled her hand away. Sorry Barry, she thought, it was time for bed-alone.

ANOTHER MONDAY

DENISE HAD nipped into the police station later that day to find out if there was an update on Cameron Stuart's shooting. There hadn't been. However, she didn't call the Dingwall police station, she was still tired from her late night.

The following day Denise was on duty with Lindsay-Joanne who was late. Again. Not very late and after the weekend they had spent she could be excused a latey.

'I'm not going to ask you if you had a good weekend,' Denise said.

L-J answered with a big smile. 'Well, yesterday was better. Scott Brown called to check I was okay because he hadn't seen me about and we spent the afternoon in bed.'

'You little minx,' Denise said.

'Stephen was asking for you, Scott said. I was nearly going to phone you.'

'No, you are all right. To tell you the truth he wasn't that good in bed.'

'Are you comparing him to the Doctor or your husband?'

'Neither. Do you think I have only had two lovers in my life?'

'No. Anyway, an average shag is better than no shag at all.'

Lindsay-Joanne was walking past the phone when it rang.

'Glenfurny police station. Detective Constable Connor speaking. Yes, she is here.'

Lindsay-Joanne shrugged as she handed over the phone, they hadn't said who they were.

'Hi. Oh, right. When did he flee?'

There was a pause and then she said- 'when?' then- 'no I am working this weekend. 'What about the follow weekend?'

She finished the call and turned to her colleague with a big smile on her face.

'I knew it. Urquart has disappeared, taking all his stuff with him. Nelson wanted to go softly softly, maybe he should have arrested him yesterday.'

'Yeah, well and good, what was the last bit, next Friday?'

Denise was close to blushing when she answered. 'Well, remember the detective that was there with D.I. Nelson, Barry, well he just asked me out.'

Lindsay-Joanne's eyes widened in disbelief. 'That's probably because I knocked him back when he asked me out on Sunday morning.'

Before Denise could say anything Lindsay-Joanne burst out laughing. 'Gotcha!'

'No, it wasn't that, I was trying to work out when he spoke to you.'

'Anyway, what about the photo in your wallet, I thought you said no more colleagues.'

'Well, apart from Stephen, nobody else is showing any interest. Anyway, it's just dinner and maybe a shag, it's not marriage.'

'That coming from the woman that called me a minx.'

The phone rang again, and Denise moved towards it.

'That will be Barry saying he has made a mistake, and he is looking for your beautiful assistant.'

'Ha ha. Glenfurny Station' was all she got out being

interrupted. Apart from saying yes sir, it was a pretty one-way conversation.

When she came off the phone again she had a bigger smile on her face. 'That was Chief Inspector McKelvie congratulating us on our work on Saturday night. Went above and beyond the call of duty. He is putting us forward for some award.'

'That's great.'

'Says he will see us all next Monday, he wants us all to be available first thing in the morning. Will need to tell the rest of the crew.'

A (CHIEF) INSPECTOR CALLS

THERE WAS a strange atmosphere in the police station as they waited on the visit of the Chief Inspector. Why was he calling was on their minds, but they were scared to put it on their lips.

At nine o'clock, almost to the second the station door opened, and the Chief Inspector walked in. He turned and looked at the crew and saw all four were present.

'Good, you are all here. Mind if I have a seat,' he said, walking round the counter amongst them.

Billy got up, almost jumping out of his seat to be sociable to the top man.

'Right folks, you are probably wondering why I am here.'

The statement was rhetorical, and nobody spoke even though they didn't know the answer to his statement.

'It's the six-month stage and now it's time for me to decide where you all go.'

This was a surprise to all, suddenly they were all looking at each other, wondering where their fate lay.

'Denise, since you came here the number of murders has doubled or trebled, not what we hoped when you came here.'

Denise swallowed hard. Not for the first time she thought she was going to be asked, or even ordered, to return to Ayrshire.

The Chief looked at her with a wry smile. 'However, the standard of your work cannot be underestimated and unless you want to move to headquarters in Inverness we are happy that you stay here in Glenfurny.'

All eyes were now on Denise.

'Sir, I am quite happy to stay here,'

'Right, I thought you would say that. Billy.'

All eyes turned to Billy, who suddenly looked nervous.

'Denise has explained your circumstances, and you will stay here with her.'

Billy smiled nervously.

'Detective Constable Connor, like the rest of the team your work has been assessed as very good. There is an opening in Dingwall for you starting next month. Cadet Susan Maxwell, your probation is over, and we want to bring another cadet in for Denise to mentor. There is a post for you back at your local station in Inverness.'

There was a silence after McKelvie spoke as what he said sank in. After all, when the boss spoke you took it as read.

'Sir,' Lindsay-Joanne spoke, 'could I request to stay here.'

The Chief Inspector looked at her as if she was speaking a foreign language. Just as he was about to open his mouth to answer he was interrupted.

'Sir, I would also like to request to stay,' Susan Maxwell said.

McKelvie looked from one to another then over at Denise. 'This is a rare occurrence. Not only has my decision ever been questioned once, here I have it questioned twice. Before deciding where you were going in your careers ladies I put a lot of thought into it. I thought surely you would want back to civilization, places like Dingwall and Inverness which had a nightlife which you young people would enjoy.'

Before continuing he looked at both in turn, but didn't get the reaction he hoped for.

'However, if you are keen to stay here I will delay any transfers for another six months.'

Nothing was said, but two ladies stifled their pleasure.

'Right, now that we have settled that get the kettle on, I'm dying for a cup of tea,' the big boss said.

DATE NIGHT

DENISE WAS allowed the choice for their date night dinner with Barry Neal and elected for the Highland Hydro. She took the bus and wondered if it would be the last bus or a taxi home, or a room for the night again.

Barry was already waiting for her in the bar and quickly finished his drink to escort her into the dining room.

'You look lovely tonight,' Barry said.

'I always look nicer after I shave,' she replied, giving him something to think about.

The head waiter showed them to their table. It was mostly couples in the room, two to a table, the majority like them in their thirties or younger.

As they were pondering their menus another couple arrived, and the guy was a bit loud. Ordering champagne, but by clicking his fingers noisily to get the wine waiters attention.

'Bubbly,' he cried out, 'and none of your cheap crap' he added.

Denise thought her meal was adequate. That said a lot about the date, a good date and the quality of the food is inconsequential, when you spend the date judging the quality of it then the meal is more important than who you are with.

By the time the dessert was placed in front of her Denise had decided Barry wasn't sharing her bed that night. Whether he knew it or not was of little interest to her, she was just hoping she made the last bus back to Glenfurny.

As Denise put the last spoonful of chocolate pudding in her mouth a sudden silence fell around the room. Looking round she saw the loudmouth who ordered the champers getting down on one knee.

Don't say yes, Denise silently begged the woman, he is a wind bag. Once again, and surprisingly, she was right.

The guy looked up expectantly then opened a ring box and popped the question. The woman screamed- no- then ran out of the dining room. A hush remained in the room until the jilted fiancée got up and fled after his intended.

Suddenly everybody looked round in silence to anyone who would make eye contact, hoping that somebody could explain what was going on, what had gone so wrong that the girl would not accept the man's proposal. Nobody had the answer it seemed.

'What do you think of that? Barry asked.

'Well, I wish I had done the same when my husband proposed to me' Denise replied.

'You are married,' he said.

'Yes, aren't you?' she came back with.

'No.'

Denise looked at her watch. 'Well, I need to be going, or I will miss my last bus.'

'But I thought,' was all he got to say.

Denise got up and walked out the restaurant. She had to move, or she would really miss the last bus.

As she walked out of the hotel she expected to see the couple who had left before her arguing or at least he would be trying to persuade her to accept his ring. All she saw was a red mini speeding out of the car park. Even from the distance she was sure there were two people in it.

The bus stop was straight across from the hotel, and she walked quickly across the car park.

Standing alone she looked over to the front of the hotel and saw a couple of staff out looking, obviously for the missing couple.

Just at that the bus drew up. After paying she sat on the side of the bus that looked out toward the hotel. The two staff members were joined by someone who appeared to be the manager.

Denise clicked her fingers; it dawned on her- it was all a scam to get a free meal. Her next case had just appeared in front of her.

ENGAGED IN A NEW CASE.

MONDAY MORNING and Denise was on duty with Susan Maxwell. The only thing passed on from the weekend was an ongoing neighbour's dispute over a hedge. More like the humdrum life Denise hoped for when she left Ayrshire for the Highlands.

As she drank her first cuppa Denise told Susan about her date and the attempt at an engagement which she felt was a con.

'Right, let's go,' she said when she finished her tea, 'we are going to the Highland Hydro.'

Denise let Susan drive the panda car. She had been on the police advanced driving course a few weeks before but struggled to get to drive when she was on with Billy.

The hotel was busy when they got there, people checking out after a weekend stay and others arriving to use the swimming pool, the only one for miles around.

When she finally got attention she asked for the manager. The snooty receptionist asked what it was about but changed her attitude when Denise showed her warrant card.

The receptionist looked past Denise and saw Susan who had her uniform. She must have pressed a buzzer on the desk because the manger appeared from his office next to the reception desk instantly and invited the two policewomen in.

'How can I help you?' he asked.

Denise was sure it wasn't the same guy who was on duty on Saturday night, she might need to come back.

'Saturday night I was in the dining room and saw what I think was a con to get free food and drink.'

'You must be talking about the fake engagement.'

'Oh, you heard about it.'

'Yes, the duty manager left all the details and left it up to me to decide whether to report it to yourselves.'

'What did you decide?' she asked him with a smile.

'To be honest, I wasn't going to bother. You are never going to catch him, and they won't try it again.'

'I think you underestimate girl power. Here we are investigating a crime before it's even been reported, that's how good we are.'

The manager smiled now. 'Okay, all we have is he booked the table under the name Tom Cooper and used a payphone, couldn't leave a phone number as they were staying at the caravan park.'

'Tom Cooper, eh, sounds like a bit of a comedian. Right, we will get the ball rolling. Obviously if you get compensation it will take weeks, maybe months. Our main aim now is to find out if they have done it before and stop anyone else from being defrauded.'

'Okay, thank you. I am sure you will let us know when you solve it.'

Back in the car Denise told Susan not to start the car for a minute. 'What's our next move?'

'Find out if they have done the same thing anywhere else.'

'Correct. Right, let's get back to the station and get onto the phones. My guess is they have been doing it somewhere else, possibly Dingwall or Inverness. There aren't many decent eateries around here, they splashed out on champagne and steaks, so they aren't going to go to a small restaurant.'

'Where would you go?'

'Good question Susan. To tell you the truth the only place I have eaten at is the Highland Hydro. Where would you go with your fellow?'

Susan thought about it. 'If money was no object we would go to Camberlee House.'

Denise looked at her as if she had just solved the 64,000-dollar question. She had heard about Camberlee House but never thought she would ever afford to eat there.

'Right, let's go there next.'

Camberlee House was an imposing mansion in it's own grounds. Left Glenfurny House looking like a pensioner's bungalow.

'God, they might charge us for parking in their grounds,' Denise said.

As they walked towards the front of the house one of the staff appeared and was going to send them round to the tradesmen's entrance when he saw Susan's uniform.

'Oh, is something wrong?'

'No, we just need to talk to the restaurant manager.'

'Right, come in and I will get her.'

The stood in the hallway of the grand building taking in the opulence of the place until the manageress appeared.

'Hi, how can I help?'

She was thin, pretty and probably in her early 40's. Denise reckoned she must be a smart cookie to hold a top job like that in a man's world.

'We are investigating a spate of thefts from restaurants. A couple eat all the best food, champagne, then he goes down on one knee. She refused his offer and runs out. He follows shortly after then they drive off.'

The manageress started laughing. 'Oh, that's cute.'

'It's not cute for the small restaurants who struggle to make ends meet. Not like here,' Denise chided her.

'No, you are right. So, what do you want to know?'

'Well, I take it they haven't been here.'

'No.'

'Here is my card. Now this time the guy booked the table in the name of Tom Cooper. Could be he uses that name all the time or he might use other comedians, you know thinking he was funny. If you get any bookings like that could you call me immediately.'

'Sure. You know I would like to meet the couple,' she said, smiling again.

'So would we,' Denise said.

In the car again, this time Susan spoke. 'Ma'am, are you sure you aren't making too many assumptions? We haven't verified they have done this anywhere else. Then there is the comedian thing, maybe his name is Tom Cooper.'

'You think he used his own name?'

'Maybe, maybe not.'

'You are right, I may be putting two and two together and getting more than four, but what I witnessed was a polished performance. The guy was loud, wanted to be seen. Then within seconds they were in the car and off. Slick. Tell you what, I will bet you lunch that I am correct.'

'Okay, as long as it's not here. It would take a month or two of my wages to get coffee and cake here.'

Susan came off the phone with a disappointed look in her face.

'What?' Denise said.

'What do you want for lunch?' she asked.

'Where?'

'The Dingwall Station Hotel three weeks ago.'

They spent the rest of the morning phoning round and totted up nine hotels they had scammed. The others they hadn't been to yet were warned of the scam and asked to phone them, or their local nick if they were suspicious.

Meantime Denise and Susan ate their lunches, macaroni pies and iced fingers courtesy of Susan in the station.

'What are you doing on Saturday night?' Denise asked.

'Fancy a night out?'

'No, I fancy our scammers will be eating out on Saturday night again. They haven't missed a good meal in the last eight weeks or nine weeks, why stop now?'

'What's the plan?'

'I would think we will need three of us. Billy can do Saturday and Sunday on his own. We do nightshift on Saturday. If we don't get a phone call from any of the hotels or restaurants we have a girly night in.'

'I'm in.'

AN ENGAGING NIGHT, OR NOT

DENISE ARRIVED at the police station just before Billy was due to clock off.

'Quiet day Bill?' she asked.

'Bit of a barney at the caravan park, but it was over by the time I got there.'

'Hope you didn't hang about until it all calmed down.'

'No, I was straight in the Escort and down there in five minutes.'

'Okay, I believe you, millions wouldn't. Any messages?'

'Yes, on the desk there.'

Denise picked it up. Cambelee House Ronald Barker eight o'clock.

'Yes,' she simply said after she read it. 'Okay Billy, off you go.'

'It's ten minutes early.'

'Okay, I am here now and the other two will be here shortly. Off you go.'

Billy looked reluctant but ceded and left.

Susan and Lindsay-Joanne walked in together. Susan wasn't wearing her uniform, orders of Denise.

'Good news, we are on. Cambelee House, eight o'clock a Mister Ronnie Barker and his fiancée not to be.'

'What are we going to do with these then?' Lindsay-Joanne said then the two girls each held up a bottle of white wine.

'Won't take us all night to wrap it up,' Denise said with a smile.

Denise parked the yellow peril in the car park at a quarter to eight. Susan was in the panda car parked well away from the house to provide for every eventuality.

Sure enough, just before eight o'clock, a red mini car arrived in the car park. It was reversed into place, ready for a quick getaway.

Denise waited half an hour before parking the yellow peril in front of the mini, then walked into the reception area and told the staff they were in place. They were expected and the staff had been told to let the couple leave.

Just before ten o'clock the fiancée not to be rushed out of the House and headed for the car. Quickly realising they had been rumbled she ran past the car, heading for the road out.

Susan and Lindsay-Joanne were ready for her and quickly caught and cuffed her. Ronald Barker came out less than a minute later and stopped in his tracks, looking at the yellow car blocking his escape.

'What the fuck?' he shouted, then saw Denise standing holding her handcuffs. Looking past Denise's car, she saw his partner-in-crime being led up by the other two women.

'All right, it's a fair cop,' he said, offering his wrists for the cuffs.

Susan left them and brought the panda car round.

'How did you know?' the guy said.

'I was in the Highland Hydro last week and saw your little act. So, what's it all about?'

'We did it last year for a laugh then tried it again this year.

When we got off with it again it just became a habit. The wife loved it, and it didn't cost us anything.'

'The bad news is, it will cost you a lot more now.'

'Yes, I know.'

'Starting with a night in Dingwall cells.'

'Really? Oh, shit.'

'What is your real name anyway, we have so many alias's for you?'

'It's Andrew Harkness.'

Denise snapped the handcuffs on him.

'There's no need for that,' he said.

'Andrew Harkness, I am arresting you for theft, anything you,' she said before being interrupted.

'Wait a minute, it's not theft.'

'Not theft? What do you call it?'

'It's called dine and dash.'

'You might call it dine and dash but the reality of it is what you are doing is stealing. Now, where was I? Oh, I will start again.'

She finished reading his rights and led him over to the panda car that Susan had driven round to the front of the big House.

When the husband and wife were in the back of the cop car Lindsay-Joanne joined Susan and they headed for Glenfurny station to wait for the van from Dingwall to pick the two prisoners up.

Denise made it back to the police station before the others and had the cell door wide open.

The couple were let in first and Denise told them to go in the cell.

'Come on, officer. It's not as if we are criminals.'

'Mister Harkness, that is exactly what you are,' she said.

Reluctantly they walked in and sat on the bunk together. That was when the arguing between them started. Denise could hear them blame each other.

'Susan, call Dingwall Police station, tell them we need a van to pick these two up. I am going to write up the report to pass on to the detective who is on nightshift over there tonight.'

Denise emerged from the back office thirty minutes later, only to be confronted by D.C. Barry Neal.

'I've got the report from tonight and the rest of the file. Mister and Missus Harkness have a history of what they call dash and dine, I call stealing.'

Barry took the file off her. 'Can we have a word,' he said.

'Sure.'

'In private.'

Denise turned and went back into the back office with Barry following. Inside she turned and folded her arms.

'What happened last week?' he asked.

'I told you; I had a bus to catch.'

'I thought we were getting on okay.'

'You aren't much of a detective then. I think after five minutes I realised I had made a mistake. Not you, but the fact you are a fellow officer. My husband was a cop, it wasn't going to work.'

Barry looked disappointed but never said anything else. He turned to leave but was stopped when Denise asked him another question.

'Did you book a room for the night?'

Barry stood for a second then went to move forward to

leave.

'You did. I phoned the Highland Hydro the next morning. Think I was an easy lay?'

The young detective never spoke and left without speaking.

Denise stayed in the office for a few minutes to cool down. When she went back into the front office the cop, and his two prisoners had gone.

Lindsay-Joanne had opened one of the bottles of wine. 'Get a cup girls, there are two bottles to drink before we go home.'

WHO IS CALLING?

DENISE WALKED into the police station with pies and cakes, lunch for Lindsay-Joanne and herself. It had been a quiet morning, and she had been glad to get out for a bit of fresh air.

'Think there's something wrong with the phone. Three times I answered it and there was nothing there,' Lindsay-Joanne said, 'oh and your friend phoned.'

'Who?' she asked, puzzled.

'The Chief Inspector. Wanted you personally.'

'I will try phoning him, might be at lunch though.'

She phoned, his secretary answered and put her through.

'Detective Sergeant Denise Kelly, you wanted a word, sir.'

'Yes. I just got word about the two diners who thought it was okay to leave without paying. Sterling work again.'

'Oh, it wasn't me, it was a team effort.'

'Yes, I have had a few phone calls thanking the force for getting those two, hopefully the courts will make an example of them and deter others.'

'Just doing my job, sir.'

'Anyway, when I get praise for a job done by my officers I like to pass it on.'

'Thank you sir, I will pass it on to my team.'

They said their goodbyes then Denise turned to Lindsay-Joanne. 'That was the boss congratulating us on the fake engagement couple.'

'Don't mention that. I still remember the hangover I had the next morning.'

'Yes, must have been cheap wine one of you bought.'

The conversation was interrupted by the phone ringing again.

'I will get it,' Denise said. 'Good afternoon, Glenfurny Police Station,' was all she got to say before being interrupted.

'Denise, we need to talk.'

'Who is this?'

'John, your husband.'

John, Denise thought it didn't sound like John. Anyway, he was inside.

'Are you phoning from jail?'

He laughed. It sounded like his laugh. Suddenly she was scared.

'No, my lawyer got me out on bail. Something to do with a technicality.'

'Have you been drinking?' she asked.

'I've had a wee celebratory drink. Now, I need to see you about us getting back together.'

'What? John, we won't be getting back together. Ever. Are you deranged?'

'Now dearest Denisey-weesy, you know how good we were together. We need to talk.'

'The days of talking are over.'

'No, they aren't.'

'Where are you anyway?'

'Close. Very close.'

'You keep away from me and Glenfurny. Do you hear me?' she screamed down the phone.

'See you soon,' he said then the phone went dead.

Denise put her head in her hands.

'What's going on?' Lindsay-Joanne asked.

'It's him. It's fucking John Kelly. He is out of jail and wants us to get back together.'

'Oh God, what are you going to do?'

'I will phone the Chief, see where I stand.'

'Detective Sergeant, we speak again so soon,' John McKelvie said when he answered her call.

'Sir, I am phoning about a serious matter. My husband has been released from jail and is threatening to come to see me. He sounds deranged. Sir, I am really scared.'

'So, how can I help?' he asked.

'I need protection.'

'A restraining order will take time Denise. What I might be able to do is arrange somebody to watch over you at night. I will need a bit of time; I will get back to you before close of play today. Okay.'

'Thank you sir.'

'Any luck?' Lindsay-Joanne asked when the conversation ended, and her boss had put the phone down.

'He says he might be able to get me protection until I arrange a court order. Would you mind a lodger tonight again?'

Lindsay-Joanne laughed. 'Okay, but it's your turn to buy the wine.'

Denise looked at her watch. Nearly five o'clock and the Chief still hadn't phoned her. She wanted to call him but knew how busy he was. If he said he would call her he would, she knew that for a fact.

'Listen, Lindsay-Joanne, I need to wait for this phone call. Why don't you take my car, and I will walk down to your place when he gets back to me. The clothes I got from my flat earlier are in the boot. All I need to get is the wine,' she said then handed the keys to the yellow peril.

'Okay, see you shortly,' she said, taking the keys and leaving Denise behind as she headed home.

CARAVAN OF LOVE

DENISE MADE it back to Lindsay-Joanne's caravan just before six o'clock. McKelvie had called her twenty minutes after Lindsay-Joanne had left the police station. Unfortunately, he couldn't get her help until the following evening.

Walking back down the street she was wary of every car that passed or approached even if it was on the opposite side of the road. John wouldn't have got to Glenfurny that quickly, could he? One thing Denise knew about him he was resourceful.

She picked up two bottles of wine and a bottle of vodka at the local wine shop on the way. Food had been an afterthought, since she had taken the phone call from him earlier she had lost her appetite completely.

Safe and secure down in Lindsay-Joanne's caravan she would be able to relax and maybe eat a bit of something.

When she got to the caravan she was relieved to see her car, the yellow peril, parked next to the van. Before going inside, she looked round the car to check it was sound.

Then she noticed the curtains were all drawn closed in the caravan. She wondered if L-J's latest boyfriend was over, and they wanted some privacy. No, not so early at night she thought.

Inside the living room was in darkness, the only light coming from the main bedroom at the end of the corridor.

'Hi, are you through there?' she shouted through as she put the wine in the fridge and the vodka on the worktop.

'What are you up to?' Denise asked, then walked down the

hallway. She looked into the bedroom and found it empty.

Suddenly she felt a presence behind her. Turning, she saw it wasn't Lindsay-Joanne but John Kelly, her husband.

He was unshaven and looked dirty, his clothes unkempt.

'What are you doing here?'

'I told you; we need to talk.'

'Where is Lindsay-Joanne?'

'She is in the other bedroom; she won't disturb us.'

'You haven't hurt her?'

'What, no. I am not here to hurt anybody. I've just restrained her, so we have a bit of privacy.'

'How did you find out where I was staying?'

'Well, unless you sold the car to her, it was easy to follow your yellow car. Hard to miss. Let's go through to the lounge.'

John started to walk through then had a thought, he walked round and grabbed her by the hair, forcing her through, making sure his wife couldn't ambush him. His actions suddenly had Denise fearing that she could be hurt, or worse- killed by him. After all, what he had done to Wendy Lee told her this was not the gentle man she had married.

As they reached the lounge he pushed her forward onto the couch and stepped toward the door, locking it securely then removed the key and putting it in his pocket.

'Do you want a drink, there is vodka there,' Denise asked as she rubbed at her sore scalp.

John licked his licks. 'Yes, a vodka would be nice. You are having one too,' he ordered.

'Of course, just to be sociable,' she lied.

Denise went into the cupboard and got two glasses out. It was only then she realised her hand was shaking. She managed to stop the shake as she poured him a large measure and a smaller one for herself.

'I haven't any mixers,' she said as she put the two glasses on the table that was between them.

'I take it straight,' he said, taking the glass and gulping half of it down.

'I need a touch of water in mine,' Denise said, then walked over to the sink. Confident John couldn't see her hands she tipped the vodka and filled the glass with water from the tap. She couldn't afford her wits being dimmed with alcohol. It was becoming obvious only one of them was walking from the caravan that night.

Sitting back down opposite her husband she drank from her glass that had only the slightest hint of vodka in it.

'God, that tastes good,' she lied.

'Don't piss me about, what about us?' he snapped.

'What about us?' she replied calmly.

'I want us to get back together,' he said. 'Back the way it was.'

'What here? Or do you want us to go back to Irvine?'

'Irvine. Irvine is an utter shitehole. This place is worse, this is an utter backwater, but Inverness is okay. I have my own flat there. I want you to come and share it with me?'

'What about here? I have a place here; we would be happy here.' Denise said as she poured more vodka in his practically empty glass.

All the time she was talking to him she tried to work out how to get out of there. Once free of the caravan she could get the Brown brothers to help her get Lindsay-Joanne free from the caravan. Could she stupefy him with drink? That was the plan she was working on. At that precise moment it was her only plan.

'Live here, what in the land that time forgot. No way.' After speaking he slugged another half a glass of the Russian fire water.

'Anyway, what about us? Where did it all go wrong?'

'Where John? You couldn't keep your cock in your trousers, that's where.'

'That wasn't my fault. It was her, my cadet. She was a right slut. We had a kiss and a cuddle one-night, next thing I know she is blackmailing me for sex. Said she would report me if I didn't keep having sex with her.'

'Oh, poor you.'

'No, Denise, I never enjoyed it with anybody else. It's only you I have ever loved. Please believe me. With the others it was only sex. Cyclops rules my life sometimes.'

'Honestly. Do you mean that?' Denise asked, trying to keep him talking until he passed out. 'Drink up.'

'What, no. I've drunk enough. Right, that's been long enough, the Cyclops needs to go to the tunnel of love.'

He got up and staggered a bit. For a moment Denise thought her plan was working until he grabbed her arm. The strong grip he had crushed her bicep and made her cry out.

'Plenty more where that came from if you don't play ball in the bedroom,' he threatened her then shook her.

Denise was dragged through to the bedroom. She had been trained in situations like these, although obviously not exactly like the position she was in, but the way to get out of it was to go along with what he wanted. If he wanted sex he would get sex.

In the bedroom Denise stripped off. As she did so she scanned the room, looking for weapons, or rather anything she could use as a weapon.

John staggered about as he struggled to get naked. After he took his trousers off he reached in the pocket and pulled out a large flick knife. He looked at it as if it was something he loved, then looked at her, before sitting it up on the narrow windowsill of the caravan window.

He was letting her know what she would get if she wasn't complicit.

In that moment her assessment, as a woman first and policewoman secondly, was that she was now in the kill or be killed stage. She would need to get her hands on that knife.

Naked, Denise lay on the bed. As she put her head between the pillows she thought of something else, if she went on top she could suffocate him. At least incapacitate him so she could get away.

Denise watched as her husband swayed where he stood. Then he took Cyclops in his hand.

'Time to go to work,' he said to it.

Denise rubbed between her legs, trying to prepare. It was going to be painful whatever he managed to do.

'Get me hard,' he said, falling into bed and lying beside her.

Denise reached down and cradled his balls. She thought about grabbing them and squeezing them tightly. The problem was if it didn't work, well, she had seen what he did to Wendy Lee.

His flaccid dick started to get a bit of life as she rubbed it. Then his hand reached over and headed up between her legs. His foreplay before had always been good, now it was groping, grasping, she wondered if he knew what he was looking for.

Without warning John crashed on top of Denise, taking the wind from her, leaving her panting.

'I used to make you breathless all the time,' he said laughing.

Then she felt him stabbing between her legs with Cyclops. He still wasn't hard enough to penetrate.

Denise closed her eyes and prayed. Not being a churchgoer, she didn't know who or what she was praying to all she wanted was for this to be over.

Her hand went down and tried to guide him in. It was obvious to her it wasn't happening.

'Want me on top?' she gasped out. He was still lying on top of her again making breathing difficult.

'You like that, being in charge,' he whispered in her ear, his rough beard brushing her cheek and neck rasping at her skin.

For an instant she thought she was going to be sick but managed to swallow it back down.

'You like it too, never fail to shoot,' she said hoarsely. The other thing she hoped for was that when they were married, after sex, he would turn round and fall soundly asleep. That would let her make her escape.

'Okay then, jockey away,' John said, rolling off and lying waiting for her.

Denise rubbed between her legs. She knew what she was about to do would hurt her, sex without lubrication always did, but it was, she thought, her only chance.

Cyclops still wasn't hard enough, so she rubbed it again. Lying on top she rubbed her sex along the Cyclop's shaft until she guessed it was hard enough to make its entrance.

She groaned as it slipped roughly in. Now it was in she had to keep going. She built up a rhythm, watching John's face as waves of pleasure started to course through his body.

He closed his eyes as the pleasure was building. Denise moved her hand along the bed until she reached the pillow he wasn't lying on. Grabbing it by the corner she flipped it up and dropped it on his face. She got a hand either side and pressed down as hard as she could, pushing with all her force.

Beneath her John started shouting, a muffled noise beneath

the pillow, then he reached up and grabbed her arms. His strong arms gripped, but her determination forced her to keep pushing down.

He was also trying to shake her off with his body, but she kept on, working her hips and still having sex with him. She felt it was like being on some wild bucking bronco. Only falling off could be deadly.

After a short time, Denise thought it felt like hours, but must have only been minutes, John's action calmed. Slowing until he stopped moving.

She had killed him. She lay on top of him until her breath returned to something near normal. Pulling off, she realised he had climaxed at some stage, his sperm dripping from her.

She got off the bed, wiped between her legs with the bed sheet then moved to the bottom of the bed to get her clothes.

Like some zombie, John suddenly rose from beneath the pillow.

With the pillow off him he struggled to work out what was happening. Denise abandoned her search for clothes and hurried toward the window sill. She grabbed John's flick knife. She clicked the switch, and the blade shot out.

'Don't get up, stay where you are,' she ordered.

'What the fuck?' he said, realising what was happening and moving towards her, reaching a hand out for the knife.

Denise batted the arm away. 'I am warning you; I will stab you!' she shouted.

John swung his legs round to the floor to get up.

Before his feet touched the floor Denise thrust the knife forward. John suddenly lunged at her and the knife plunged into his chest.

Denise let the knife go and pushed him back onto the bed.

'Fuck!' she screamed, then moved round the bed and grabbed her clothes. John dropped back onto the bed. Denise was suddenly sure she had killed him.

Out, she had to get out. Moving down the hall and trying to get her trousers on she realised she needed the caravan keys.

With her trousers on, but not even zipped up, she moved back into the bedroom and found his trousers.

John was lying in the same position she had left him.

Grabbing the caravan keys, she rushed to the front door of the caravan. Grabbing a jacket, she wrapped it round her.

With shaking hands, she managed to unlock the door and stepped out.

Without looking back, she hurried over the car park to the reception area. Her bare feet crunched the stones beneath, the pain not noticed as the adrenalin coursed through her veins.

Inside the reception area was deserted. She banged on the counter then saw there was a buzzer for a bell on the counter and a sign advising to ring it for attention.

She hit it, hoping somewhere it would be buzzing. After ten seconds, when no one showed up she kept dropping her hand on it. Again and again, she buzzed it until eventually the site owner turned up.

'All right calm down. Oh fuck,' he said. 'What's happened?'

The blood on Denise's hand, and all over the buzzer was evidence something terrible had happened.

'We need the police and an ambulance, Lindsay-Joanne Connor's caravan.'

'Police, are you not the police.'

'Yes, but I am involved. For Christ's sake, can you not see the mess I am in. Hurry up and phone them.'

Denise turned and walked away, heading for the Brown

brother's caravan. Stoating across the car park she was like a zombie. Her bare feet suddenly started to get sore on the sharp stones beneath her feet.

At the caravan she tried to bang on the door. However, the strength had drained from her. Her arms were like jelly after John's grip. All she could do was kick on the door.

The door opened a fraction, then opened fully. Stephen Brown stood there in a t-shirt and shorts.

'What the fuck?' he said, looking down at Denise, half naked and her right hand caked in blood.

'I need you to help Lindsay-Jo,' was all she could get out.

Stephen disappeared back into the caravan. Waiting for them Denise leaned against the caravan, trying to believe the events of the past twelve hours weren't real.

The caravan door opened again, and the two brothers appeared.

'What happened?' Scott asked.

'My husband turned up.' Denise pointed to Lindsay-Joanne's caravan. It was only then she realised her hand was covered in blood, her husbands.

'Lindsay-Joanne is tied up.'

Scott rushed off, desperate to help his girl. Stephen took Denise by the arm to help her across to the caravan.

'Come on, let's see that she is all right,' he said.

When they walked back into the caravan, Denise and Stephen found the spare room door open.

'I'll kill that bastard!' they heard Scott shout.

'Too late,' Denise said to Stephen, 'I think I've beat him too it.'

Lindsay-Joanne appeared from the room. She pointed to Denise. 'Your husband is a lunatic!' she screamed.

'Was,' Denise said. 'I think I killed him. Scott, look in to the bedroom.'

Scott let go of L-J's arm and did as he was asked, standing in the doorway and looking in.

'Fucking hell! Looks like a butcher's shop in there!' Scott shouted excitedly.

Somewhere in the distance there were sirens sounding. Help was on its way.

RECOVERY

DENISE WOKE up from the biggest nightmare of her life. She looked around her and tried to work out where she was. Hospital. She tried to sit up, but whatever they pumped into her was keeping her on her back. Next she tried to lift her arms up. Even that wasn't possible, looking at her arms she saw they were a mass of bruises.

'You are awake then,' a voice said.

She closed her eyes and tried to place the voice. Lindsay-Joanne, was it her? Opening them again she turned her head slowly to the left. It was her. She was dressed in hospital bedclothes.

'Are you okay?' Densie asked.

'Yes, but no thanks to your husband.'

Suddenly it all came flooding back to her. John had attacked her. 'Is, is he dead?' she asked.

Lindsay-Joanne looked away as she spoke. 'Yes,' was all she said. 'The police want to talk to you,' she added.

'Of course they will.'

'See you then, I am getting out shortly,' Lindsay-Joanne said, then walked away.

Just at that a nurse turned up and checked her vitals. 'You seem a lot better, Mrs. Kelly, We will have you out of here in no time.'

'Thanks,' Denise said.

Next morning the Doctor on his rounds told her she was free to go home. How would she get there, she wondered. When she got dressed she walked out to the payphone in the corridor and called the police station.

Billy answered. It was good to hear a friendly voice, she thought.

'Billy, could you do me a massive, big favour.'

There was a silence on the other end of the line.

'Billy.'

'Yes.'

'Could you do me the ultimate favour and come to Dingwall hospital and get me.'

There was a pause as Billy was obviously putting a hand over the mouthpiece of the phone as he spoke to someone.

'Yes, okay, I can come at lunchtime,' he conceded.

'Thanks Billy, top man.'

There was no reply from the other end.

Denise got dressed on what clothes she had. Somebody had obviously got some of her clothes from Lindsay-Joanne's caravan and put them in her bedside locker.

They were the clothes she had been wearing that night. Putting them on was excruciatingly painful. Every bit of her ached now the painkillers were being reduced. Her arms, each one turned into one giant bruise, ached. Her legs, which she used to keep on top of her husband felt as though she had just run a Marathon without training beforehand. Her head ached; her feet were covered in cuts from the gravel in the car park. Finally, her vagina had, according to the Doctors, had severe internal bruising, causing pain whenever she went to the toilet.

Fortunately, she had been given the morning after pill, she

didn't need to worry about that.

Christ, as she was getting dressed she didn't even know what day it was. Anyway, first thing she had to do was get out of there and back to her own bed. The thought of it cheered her.

As she sat on the bed, getting her breath back, she wondered why the police hadn't appeared by then. She knew she had to be interviewed and soon.

Walking out from the hospital entrance and into the fresh air felt great. She felt lucky to be alive. Billy wasn't waiting for her though, that wasn't like him. She thought nobody was there for her, then she saw a familiar car in the car park.

Detective Inspector Nelson got out the car when he saw her and started walking towards her. His assistant got out and followed him.

'Hi, sir,' she said when he was in front of her. 'I am just waiting on my lift.'

'You won't need it.'

'What? Why?'

'You are coming with us. Denise Kelly, I am arresting you for the murder of John Kelly. Anything you do say can and will be used as evidence.'

Whatever else Nelson said after that, she missed. She knew the script off heart anyway. Murder John, though. How could they think she would murder John? It was self-defence, surely they would know that.

She still loved him, in a way. Well, not the monster that turned up in their village, but the John Kelly she had married before he cheated on her.

Although he was dead, the bastard was still making her suffer she thought.

Nelson clapped the handcuffs on Denise's wrists making it suddenly feel very real.

'Wait, it was self-defence,' she said.

'Not when you stab somebody in the heart,' Nelson replied, then led her to his car.

THE END

Printed in Great Britain
by Amazon